Castle Of Pine

A Short Novel

Dakota Shalins

Contents

1

OUR NEW FRIEND

The sounds of birds chirping, the fresh dew from the summer fog, it was another spectacular morning for Barb Jackson. "Hi snuggles, I hope you slept well honey" said Barb, she got out of bed and began her day by taking a shower then feeding her cat Snuggles. Barb worked as the school nurse and teacher; she was ready for another day of rugrat's running around accidentally hurting themselves.

She was always determined to do great things and raise children, but love has always been hard for her. Barb got dressed and looked herself in the mirror saying her daily quote, "it's okay if today doesn't go your way, you are still a wonderful person." As if she was always anticipating something bad to happen because she lacked confidence in herself.

"Alright now where did I put my heels?" "Oh! that's right" Barb shuffled under her dresser and found them stuffed under the corner. She threw on her heels, grabbed her purse then looked at Snuggles and blew a kiss before walking out the door. Barb began to walk outside looking around at the neighbors to see if anyone was out and about, but everyone was still asleep.

She grabbed her car keys out of her purse and began to walk to her car. Barb saw a student walking down the road who looked like she might have run away from home. "Emma?" Shouted Barb "Are you okay honey?", "I'm fine" said Emma, as she cried so much, she couldn't see who even called her name.

Barb began approaching her, Emma wiped her eyes and saw it was her teacher. To Barb's surprise Emma sprinted in the other direction as fast as she could. "Emma! Where are you going! what is going on?!", "I'm fine! Leave me alone," Emma screamed then ran to the wood line until she was completely alone. She cuddled up against a tree crying uncontrollably, hugging the tree.

"Dad, I miss you, I'll never stop loving you," she said, "Mom isn't the same since you died and Steve is not my dad. He will never be my dad!" she shouted in anger. Barb looked around confused to see if anyone else was witnessing this, but again all the neighbors were asleep.

She took her heels off and ran to the woods where Emma ran to try and find her, "Emma!

Sweetie, it's me Ms. Jackson." She kept walking as the twigs and rocks made it hard to keep her footing. Barb then turned a corner and saw Emma crying and kneeled to hug her.

"It's okay child, I'm here honey don't you worry," said Ms. Jackson. "I Miss my dad, I don't know what to do," Emma replied. "I understand sweetie, but your father loves you very much and would hate to see you hurting this much," Barb said with tears in her eyes. "Well how do I move on? I don't know what to do, I can't stop crying every day and I hate my stepdad, he is not my dad," Emma said, violently shaking. "He never will be your dad honey, but you can't hate him for that. Your dad will always be your father, he is in your heart whenever you need him," Barb said. She looked Emma in the eyes wiping her tears. "Okay. Thank you" Emma replied, she then swiftly wrapped her arms around Ms. Jackson.

"I think I'm ready to go to school now," Emma stood up and took a deep breath grabbing Ms. Jackson's hand. "Okay honey let's go," they both walked back down the forest path onto the pavement. Barb opened the passenger door of her Car for Emma and shut the door behind her. Ms. Jackson got into her car and continued to drive Emma to school.

"You know you didn't have to tell me why you ran away from home, but if you ever need someone to talk to, you can trust me," Barb said. "Thank you Miss Jackson," Emma replied with appreciation in her tone. "Steve and my mom were fighting last night, it was about how I don't want to play softball, but Steve wants me to. I heard him say he would divorce my mom if I didn't start listening to him and treating him like my father." Barb looked shocked and disappointed in Steve.

"I'm sorry Emma, that sounds awful sweetie, but you can't just run away from home.", "I know but if I didn't run away, I would've woken up getting yelled at again. I just can't take it anymore. It hurts too much." Emma replied. "I understand, hey do you want to stop and get breakfast before we go to school?" said Barb. Knowing that it would make them both late, she was eager to find out what's really going on with Emma. "Sure" Emma replied. Ms. Jackson pulled into The Dingy Diner, "I don't have any money", "that's okay honey I got it." Barb said. They continued inside to the beautiful 50's themed Diner with classic rock music playing from the jukebox.

"Aren't we going to be late to school?" Emma said concerned. "Yes, slightly, don't worry honey, I'll take care of it," Barb replied. "Hey Barb, two for here?" said the waitress, "yes please," Barb pointed at Emma to follow the waitress. They sat down and began to order their food until Steve pulled into the Diner looking for Emma.

He slammed his truck door with frustration walking towards the door and saw Emma with Barb. "Miss Jackson what are you doing with my daughter at a Diner when she is supposed to be at school?" Steve said angrily. "I saw her walking down the road and offered her a ride to school. We decided to stop at the diner for a bite to eat first," Barb replied. Steve grabbed Emma by the arm as she was about to talk and pulled her out of the booth. He then pointed at Barb, "I will talk to the principal about this, Emma get in the car now." Emma looked Ms. Jackson in the eye with sorrow and went outside to the car.

After Steve and Emma left, Barb looked out the window watching him scream at her, as if she had just done the worst thing imaginable, "poor girl," Barb said. "Waitress can I get the bill please", "you got it Barb one moment." After a shifty morning, Barb arrived at Thorn Oak Middle School. Anxious and ready for any type of disruption that was ahead of her.

As she walked in Steve was just about to leave and walked past her, "good luck" he said with a smug face. "Here we go," Barb said to herself as she walked in ready to brave the news. She went directly to the principal first thing. "Hi Miss Jackson having a good day?" said the principal, "Yes am I in trouble?" she replied. "Not that I know of," he said as he walked away. Barb turned around with a raised brow and proceeded to her classroom that she was already twelve minutes late for.

"Good morning class how are we all today?", "Great" said Harold, "I just farted" said Noah, "grow up" Emma responded. "Alright let's do our morning attendance," Ms. Jackson said. She continued her daily routine without worrying about what happened earlier.

The next day Emma woke up, remembering what Miss Jackson had spoken to her about. She was grateful for their conversation. Emma got out of bed, she didn't hear fighting so her parents must be sleeping still. She scurried downstairs and made her breakfast quietly, hoping not to wake them. Taking it back to her bedroom upstairs and getting ready for school.

Emma loved her long brown hair and always thought it was her best trait. Her big brown eyes were a close second favorite. She wasn't a very sociable kid ever since her father had died in a horrific car crash four years ago. Although she was extremely loving and sharp.

Growing up in Elvingdale there wasn't much to do other than ride her bike or hang out in the backyard with her dog. Emma picked up a passion for art that kept her mind busy, so she wasn't afraid to be alone. Her art consisted of portraits of her father holding her as a baby or bringing her to the mall. After she was done eating and getting ready, she grabbed her backpack and a few dollars from Steve's wallet, then left in a hurry.

Almost every week she would make sure to go visit her father's grave which was on the way to school. It was always helpful for her to feel like she could still talk to him even though he was dead. Emma neared his grave and she began to pray. "Thank you god for giving me life and for keeping me safe and healthy," then she walked over to her dad's grave. She sat next to him, running her hands through the grass as if it was her father's hair. "I love you dad, don't ever forget it" she said. She rubbed her hands together then stood up and made her way back to the road.

Emma thought as long as she kept visiting him, he would visit her and protect her. Emma arrived at school five minutes before class, "Hey Emma," said Josie Jean. "Hey Josie, is Ms. Jackson here yet?", "yea she is inside", "okay thanks!" Emma replied. "Emma…do you want to hangout sometime?" Josie said shakily. After all, she didn't have many friends and lived with her adoptive family. "Of course! Do you want to come over to my house after school?" Emma replied, with a big smile on her face. "I'd love to! See you after class," Josie walked away shining with glee.

Class was starting but Josie walked to the hallway and opened her locker to find a pencil. She found a strange piece of paper inside that looked like it was a note. She picked it up, "Josie your eyes shine brighter than the stars," Josie looked over her shoulder to see who could have left the note. She stuttered, folding it up, throwing it in her pocket. Josie Shut her locker and found her way to the classroom. All Josie could think was, "I found a new friend and a boy from school likes me? this can't be true…." she continued pinching herself to make sure she was awake. "Well…I guess it must be true, awesome!" Josie sat down in her chair and looked around the classroom.

Harold sat down to her left and Noah sat to her right. "Could it be one of them?" she thought, neither of them seemed to even glance her way. Josie opened her schoolbook, "Welcome back class! It's great to see you all again. I hope you had an easy time with last night's homework assignment on division and multiplication tables. I look forward to seeing all your work, if you could please bring up your assignments now and drop them in the bin." said Miss Jackson.

Harold shot up like a rocket and started playing air guitar with his sheet of paper. "Sweet Love of Miiieiiineee…. Oooo," the whole class started to laugh, including Ms. Jackson. "Heck yeah Harold, kick it!" Noah said, with his pencil banging against the desk creating percussion. "Alright ha-ha thank you boys for the show, but keep it a little quieter please", "yes Miss Jackson," Harold replied.

Harold tossed the paper in the bin and went back to his chair. Once Noah sat down Harold whispered, "Hey want to come over tonight? We can play with checkers or Atari. My mom bought me a new one after the last one stopped working", "Sure bro, talk later," Noah replied. Noah grabbed his pencil and began jotting down whatever Ms. Jackson was saying. Halfway through class the students would all get one hour to go outside, run around and eat lunch. Thorn Oak Middle School doesn't have the biggest yard, but it was enough to cater the students and allow enough space to run around.

There is a big oak tree in the middle, with swings to the left and a basketball court to the right. Everyday Harold would challenge Charleston or Evan to a game of H-O-R-S-E to see who the better shot is. Whoever lost had to give the winner a quarter and do one lap around the basketball court. It's safe to say that Harold wasn't the best player. In fact, the best player at the school was Evan but Evan only wanted to watch most of the time.

Evan came from a family of Military Generals and Royalty on his mom's side, yet he has no idea about any of it. He was adopted at the age of one and always wanted to grow up and meet his parents. As he got older, he couldn't stop thinking, "how could someone abandon their baby?" Because of that Evan would only play basketball when he was very angry.

"Pass the brick" Charleston said, looking at Harold. "Bring it Charleston, I'm going to mop the floor with you," Harold took the first shot. "Swish! uh oh" he said, as Charleston lined up to repeat the shot Harold just took. Charleston lifted the ball above his head and took a shot, "Airball!" Harold screamed, followed by a goofy giggle.

The next shot was up to Harold and just like the last one, "swish! huh...I'm on fire!" Harold said. "Yea I wish you were on fire, literally so I could win this game right now," Charleston whispered. "What did you say bro?" Harold asked. "Uh…umm...nothing," Charleston took a shot and again, "Airball!" screamed Harold. This time Charleston just couldn't deal with the pressure; he grabbed the basketball and threw it over the fence into the woods. "You want to win so badly? go grab the ball then!" Harold was confused. He thought Charleston knew he was just joking around, Harold shrugged it off and hopped the fence.

"Ouch!" Harold snagged the fencing and cut his finger open. He was still determined to get the basketball because it was his favorite thing to do at school. Harold kept walking deeper into the woods, in the direction of the ball. He heard faint sounds in the distance; He started to panic and became vigilant to his surroundings. "It's probably just an animal or something," Harold said. He saw the ball down the hill on the edge of the creek. He shuffled his feet like a penguin to avoid losing his balance slowly making his way down the deeply slanted hill.

All a sudden the wind picked up and the smell of dead flesh took over the air. "Ew something definitely died here, somewhere," Harold said. He bent over to grab the ball, and heavy footsteps began shaking the ground. A loud bell kept ringing, *Ding, Ding*, Harold freaked out, he looked around and saw nothing. The footsteps kept getting louder and louder, "HELP! Someone help me!" Harold started screaming.

He grabbed the basketball and ran up the hill as fast as possible. "This isn't real, this isn't real," once he could see the fence again, he froze and suddenly the ground stopped shaking. The bell stopped ringing and the footsteps stopped moving. He couldn't see anything as his eyes peered at the trees; he turned back towards the court and hopped the fence.

"You okay bro? we heard you screaming," said Charleston. "Yeah…I'm…okay," Harold said. "What could that have been?" he said to himself. Harold shrugged it off and got back to the game. "Break time is over, please get back to class," the intercom startled Harold, he dropped the ball from fear and froze. All the other kids started walking back inside the school. Harold felt what he just witnessed was real even though it stopped. He continued walking inside and went back to his seat.

Josie looked over at him and smiled wondering if it still could have been him who left the note. "Hmm Josie is acting weird today…today is strange," Harold thought to himself. He opened his binder and grabbed his schoolwork. After class finally came to an end Noah looked over at Harold, "hey man can I still come over later?", "I forgot my mom is bringing me to the mall. Sorry maybe tomorrow?", "oh. Okay yea that works!" Noah replied. Harold was still scared and needed more time to himself to figure out what was going on with him.

All the students rushed out of class to head home except for Emma. She walked up to Ms. Jackson, "Hey, thank you again for the talk we had. It really meant a lot to me," Emma said. "Of course, sweetheart! Was your morning better today?", "yes it was, thank you, I'll see you tomorrow.", "Do you want a ride home?" Ms. Jackson replied. "No, I'm okay, I'm going to stop at my father's grave again on the way home. "Okay well stay safe, see you tomorrow, Emma!", "bye," Emma waved goodbye and left the classroom into the hallway. She saw Josie waiting for her and she smiled, "Hi Josie, ready?" Josie waved, "yes! let's go!" she replied and they started walking down the street to the mall.

The girls held each other's hands and started singing. The girls laughed and found their way to the mall entrance. "Now I got some of my stepdad's money, so let's go buy some new clothes for you," Emma said. "Oh, okay what's wrong with mine?" Josie replied, with her cute little cowgirl boots, jean shorts and her tattered checkered shirt. "Nothing is wrong with your clothes, but wouldn't you like to have some more girly clothes?" Emma said. "I guess so…I've never worn a dress before,", "See! girl let's get you what you deserve," Emma said while holding the door open for Josie. They entered the mall looking around to make sure no one from school was there.

Sapphire Mall had a big fountain in the middle with an orange smoothie shop in the left corner. "Ooo… I want a smoothie first!" Josie said, "okay!" Emma replied. Josie and Emma got their smoothies and sat down to drink them.

"Do you always walk to school?" Josie asked while slurping down her smoothie. "Yes, I mainly walk to school because Steve is the only one who can bring me and I don't really like him, so I prefer walking," Emma replied. "Oh, okay that makes sense, does your mom still work the night shift?" Josie asked. "Yeah, she gets home right before I get up and goes to bed, I try not to bother her or make too much noise,", "It's got to be hard working overnight," Josie stated. "I'm sure it's very tiring," Emma replied.

The girls were finally bonding for the first time after being in the same class for three years. They finished their smoothies and threw the cups in the trash. "Alright Josie let's go get you a super cute dress, so all the boys at school lose their minds" Emma said. Josie seemed smitten by the idea, "I'd love that," they grabbed each other's hands. They continued walking over to the clothing store to find Josie a beautiful new dress.

Josie wasn't much of a girly girl; she spent most of her days jumping in the mud and playing with the local pond frogs. She was abandoned by her parents when she was a little girl and ever since then she lived with the Lacey's in a small blue house. It wasn't very big or very comfortable, but it was a home. A place where she could at least be happy and dance around.

Emma stopped and turned, "Oh! we should go into here first and get some earrings," Emma said. "Yes queen!" Josie replied. "Welcome girls" the cashier said. "Hi" Emma replied, "let's get you some big hoop earrings", "I've never worn those before…" Josie replied shyly. She didn't know how to feel, she never dressed very girly before.

David Lacey's mom wasn't very girly herself; she worked at a local farm with animals all day, so she was mainly covered in mud. Some days she would come home and take a shower and literally do nothing for the rest of the night. She was exhausted, Josie didn't blame her, but she wished that they could bond more.

"I like these ones!" Josie picked up a pair of shiny silver hooped earrings, "these are the ones, I love them," she said. "Okay let's get you those then!" Emma replied. Emma grabbed them from her and walked up to the cashier, "just these please!", "You got it," said the cashier. "Would you like a bag?", "no that's okay, I'll just put them in my backpack," Josie said. "Have a good day you two,", "you as well!" Emma replied.

The girls found their way out of the store and back into the mall center. "Thank you Emma, I love them,", "no problem! now let's get you that dress," Emma said. The girls went back to the clothing store and started jumping with excitement. They entered the store and looked around "how about this one?", "Too plain," Josie said. "This one?", "Eh I don't like the color", "okay" Emma replied. She was determined to find the right dress that Josie would love. "This one is very shiny and silver and would go perfect with those earrings," Emma said. She held up the dress for Josie to see, "oh my god…it's gorgeous! I want that one!" Josie replied, with a smile bigger than her heart.

The girls proceeded to pay for the dress and walked out of the store. They ran into Evan, "oh...uh...hi Evan," Emma waved. Josie clenched up and started blushing. Evan waved and walked away into the boy's store. Josie couldn't believe that she had forgotten to tell Emma about the note she found in her locker.

"Emma how did I forget to tell you. I found a letter in my locker this morning, it said my eyes shine brighter than the stars, but it didn't say who it was from," Emma was in shock but replied, "oh my... maybe it was him!", "I have no idea who it was, it's been killing me to find out. I kept waiting for one of them to come up to me or talk to me in class. No one said anything, so I really don't know what to think," Josie said. "They must be very shy or embarrassed, after all boys think we have cooties,", "ha-ha isn't that funny? I can't get over how silly boys are," Josie giggled.

"Tomorrow, wear that dress. I guarantee whoever left that note in your locker won't be able to resist talking to you," Emma said. "Yes! That's a great idea. Thank you again, I'm having so much fun hanging out with you," Josie replied. "Don't mention it! I'm just happy to help, why didn't we hang out sooner?!", "I don't know…I'm shy", "awe that's okay Josie, but you don't have to be shy around me!" Emma stated. "I know I just can't help myself; I don't really know why I'm so awkward," Josie replied.

Ever since Josie was abandoned, she never could find confidence. She couldn't express herself fully without feeling out of place and like she didn't belong. "I'll admit since my dad died, I haven't been very outgoing or feeling like myself anymore either," Emma admitted. The girls seemed to have a similar feeling of pain from trauma that they could both relate to.

"Oh no! It's getting late," Josie said abruptly. "I got to go back home before mom gets home," Josie stuffed the dress in her backpack and zipped it up. "Okay let's get out of here!" Emma said. They ran out of the mall, hugged each other goodbye and parted ways. "Bye Emma see you tomorrow!", "You too Josie, have fun trying the dress on,", "oh I will!" Josie replied. Emma found herself smiling and started walking to her father's grave.

2

CHATTERBOX

"Momma, where is my gator tooth necklace? I can't seem to find it", "I don't know, maybe look in the couch cushions or maybe look under em." said Momma Tree. She stood six feet of pure muscle. Harold lifted open a jar of cookies. As soon as he grabbed one, he already knew he would need another.

"First focus on the necklace I want to wear today then we can focus on the cookies," he chuckled. "Baby don't be eating that many cookies in one day you're going to get sick. We can't have that, you got to be tough for this year's basketball try outs,", "Yes momma," Harold replied. He snuck a second cookie in his mouth, closed the lid and went back searching for the missing necklace.

Momma Tree had a very thick accent and whenever she spoke it sounded like she had peanut butter stuck to the roof of her mouth. This was Harold's favorite trait about her, Other than being a fierce, strong lady who didn't have a single second for nonsense. Harold eventually found his necklace hanging outside on the table that fit their cute patio perfectly. He snatched it and proceeded to put it over his head, "alright alright…It's me, the gator man," he said comedically.

Harold was always the life of the party wherever he went, no matter how humbug someone else was, he always made them smile. Harold went back inside, "alright bye Momma time for me to go to school and make some sick rifts", "baby we talked about this, no air guitar in school. You need to pay attention and learn,", "yeah…I know…Okay. Bye!" Harold dashed out the door and waited for the school bus. Harold didn't live far from school. He normally would walk or ride his bike, but it was one of those days when he felt lazy and complacent.

The bus arrived and Harold saluted the bus driver as he walked on. "Good morning, student 8 reporting for duty", "Good morning, Harold, take a seat," the bus driver closed the door and drove off. "Morning Charleston, are you ready for another showdown today? Or do you want to have a concert in class instead?" Harold said. Charleston was too tired to comprehend what Harold had said. "Yeah bro I don't know, I might just chill today," Charleston replied.

Harold gazed out the window as the bus arrived to pick up David. "Uh oh here comes Jabba the Gut," Harold cackled. "Hey man, that's our friend, be nice," Charleston replied. "I'm only kidding bro…", "Yeah well you are a chatterbox, and it gets annoying," Charleston muttered. "Hey guys what's up?" David said. "Hey bro," Charleston replied. The bus finally made it to the school and they all hopped off.

"Chatterbox? Do I really talk that much? Am I really that annoying? I thought we were cool," Harold said to himself before walking to class. Ms. Jackson wrote, "Good morning class," on the board and waited for the class to start. The school alarm rang for class to begin, and everyone made their way to their seats. "Hello everyone, today we will be starting a new lesson on Force and Motion. I'm going to be passing out these books for you to take home and study for next week. We will take a test next Thursday, so be ready." The kids all groaned and moaned and seemed unenthused.

"Okay open up your books to chapter one and begin reading for the first hour of class today, take notes," Ms. Jackson said. Josie looked at the boys in the room and waited to see if anyone noticed her shiny silver dress and new earrings. She didn't see anyone notice, so she hung her head and went back to reading. "Hubba, hubba," Harold said to himself as he looked over at Josie. Evan sat at the front of the room and began to take notes. While taking notes pencil broke and needed to be sharpened. He got up and walked to the back of the classroom.

He saw Josie Jean with her curly hair and sparkly dress, and he instantly fell in awe. Evan started sharpening his pencil, "should I say something…do I let her know…?" he kept sharpening until his pencil was nearly a nub. Josie looked at him, "hey are you done yet?", "oh…uh…yes, I'm done. By the way…you look beautiful today…I mean. You always look beautiful! but the dress...wow," Evan said. He was stumbling over his words. Josie Blushed, "Thank you so much," she said before giggling. Evan went back to his seat and kept reading until it was time for break.

Most of the kids went outside for recess, but Evan went to the bathroom this time and washed his face. "Oh my god she is beautiful, but I can't talk to her. I don't know what to say when I see her," he said to himself in the mirror. He walked outside and saw Josie was outside swinging with Emma. "Girl, you won't believe it…Evan just told me I look beautiful today," Josie said. "Oh my god! Emma replied before gasping. "Did he say he left you the note?", "no but It's got to be him right? I mean he looked shocked when he saw me!" Josie said. She was swinging higher with a big smile on her face. "Thank you again for buying me the dress and earrings, you're the best Emma", "awe Josie you're welcome, don't mention it!" Emma replied.

The girls kept swinging while the boys were on the other side sitting on the basketball court, talking. "Man, Josie is smoking today," Harold said. "Hey bro, have some respect," Charleston replied. "You both wouldn't have a chance anyway," Evan said with a big smirk on his face. "Yeah bro, you think so huh?" Harold laughed. "I mean you are probably right, but she looks good", "yes she does," Evan replied. "Guys what is David doing?" Charleston observed, He couldn't help but notice David walking into the woods and disappearing down the hill.

Harold immediately froze and thought to himself, "oh no, not him too," David started walking down the hill with a sad look on his face. He heard a frog, *Ribbit, Ribbit,* "where are you at, I'm going to get you," David said. He started looking in the water and couldn't see anything other than his own reflection looking back at him. He got down on his knees, it sounded so close, like it came from the mud just under his hands. David looked down at the water, quickly shooting his hands into the mud, "Darn it. no frog," he said with a handful of mud. David started to wash his hands when the ground started to shake, the trees started to bend and the screeches of the unknown started howling.

"What…what is going on?" he got back up to the hillside when he tripped over a stump and fell backwards. He was looking up at the tree canopy, they violently swooshed back and forth, the sounds kept getting louder and louder. David gathered himself, got up and ran up the hill. "This isn't real," he said, as he stood at the top gasping for breath. "Guys, David looks scared or something," said Charleston. Harold couldn't help but wonder, "did he just experience the same thing as I did?" The boys all ran over to the fence that David was leaning on to see if he was okay or not.

"Hey bro what happened?" Charleston said. "I am not sure guys," David replied, breathing heavily. "Did you hear anything?" Harold said, David looked at him and stopped breathing. "I heard something," David said, gripping the fence with force. "Yeah, I heard it the other day," replied Harold. "What are you guys talking about?" Charleston replied. David and Harold looked at each other, they both disregarded the event, "nothing" Harold said. Little did any of the boys know this was the start of a horrifying adventure.

"Emma, what are the boys even doing right now?" Josie said, while pointing at them yonder. "I don't really know. I guess something must've happened to David, he looks like he is crying,", "oh, I hope he is okay. Should we go and check on them?", "Josie, those boys are fine, don't worry about them." Emma replied. She continued swinging her little heart out, hoping she could touch the stars.

"I feel like I could swing all the way around,", "Yea right Emma, please don't try that," Josie replied. "I won't...I won't...I'm just kidding," the girls laughed. The school bell rang and all the children halted their activities. "Let's go back to class guys," David said then he hopped the fence. Charleston and Harold helped him wipe the dirt off his clothes. Harold swung his arm over David, "I got you brother, don't worry we will figure out what's going on," he said. Harold pulled his arm back and then walked inside the school.

They arrived at the classroom, sat down and listened to Ms. Jackson. "Okay welcome back, I hope you all had a good time outside and didn't get into too much mischief," The boys looked at each other and grinned. "I hope to see you all pass this test on Force and Motion next week with flying colors," Ms. Jackson said. Most of the kids all had good grades in class, but Harold found himself struggling to keep up. He always tried his best in school, but his mind would tend to wonder.

Harold looked out of the school windows and saw a crow fly into the big oak tree in the yard. The crow cawed and cawed distracting him from paying attention to Ms. Jackson's lesson. He began fixating on the sound piercing into his head, when the crow suddenly flew over to the tree line. Harold was about to look away when randomly, the bird dropped to the ground midflight and stopped moving.

Harold became paralyzed with emotions and confusion; it was like the crow hit something invisible in the air and fell to its death. "Ms. Jackson, may I go to the bathroom please?" he asked. "Of course, take the bathroom stick," she replied. Harold got up, grabbed the stick and crept into the hallway scanning the corridor.

He didn't see any teachers, only one student at the sink, so he dashed out of the back door into the schoolyard. He sprinted over to the fence and looked around for the bird. He couldn't see it, so he hopped over the fence. Harold kept hearing the cawing in his head, beating, as if it was right next to him and then he found the crow. The bird was on the ground with its head missing and the rest of its body remaining. He was disgusted, he took a breath in and quickly hopped back over the fence heading back into school.

Harold was freaking out, but he also knew he couldn't get caught. He waited outside the classroom for a second, closed his eyes and then opened the door. "Welcome back," Ms. Jackson said. Harold smiled and walked quickly back to his chair. "Bro are you okay?" Charleston asked, "No I'm not, talk after class," Harold replied. "Oh great, did you see another UFO or something? you're always seeing crazy stuff," Charleston chuckled. "For your information, UFO's do exist, but no, not this time I got evidence. I'll show you after class," Harold responded.

The end of the day started to near and the students all became hangry, shaking their legs waiting to go home. "Alright class that's everything for today, have a good rest of your night everyone and see you next week!" Ms. Jackson said. "You too," Josie responded. "I hope you have a great weekend Ms. Jackson," Emma said, smiling from ear to ear. Harold grabbed his backpack and made his way out of the classroom to find David waiting in the hallway next to Charleston. "Where is this proof you want to show us huh?" Charleston asked.

"This way boys, follow me!" Harold replied. They walked onto the basketball court and put their backpacks down near the fence.

"Okay, hop over guys," Harold said. "I'm not going back in there," David replied. "No don't worry, it's not that far,", "oh okay," David and Charleston hopped the fence and followed Harold. "Right over here guys," Harold got closer to the spot where he saw the crow, but he couldn't find it.

He took a second look around to make sure he wasn't in the wrong spot, but now he was sure that this was indeed the spot. "Hey bro what are you looking for?" David asked. Harold was shocked that the crow was gone, he didn't understand how. "Maybe an animal grabbed it? yeah that had to be it," he said to himself.

"There was a crow right here on the ground with its head cut off and I watched it fall from the sky while it was flying. I swear it was here! I know it was," Charleston and David looked at each other, concerned. "Bro, you're losing your mind I swear, you need to go see a doctor or something," Charleston said. Harold repeated himself frantically, "It was here! I know it," David looked at him and thought he was telling the truth.

After what David had been through earlier, he thought anything was possible at this point. "I doubt it, you're just making this stuff up, I'm going home," Charleston said. David looked at Harold, sighed and walked back to the fence. "I don't get it" Harold said to himself, looking at the grass hoping the bird would just reappear.

He paced back and forth for a few minutes thrashing his feet into the tall grass. He was hoping the crow was hidden underneath somehow but had no luck. Harold gave up, accepting defeat, he grabbed his backpack and plodded home.

3

The Crow

September 10th. 1988

The weekend began like any other for Harold except he felt a bit groggy and unwell, getting out of bed Saturday morning. Harold stretched his arm to the ceiling and took a gander out of his window to his wooded backyard. Hoping he could see the birds that were chirping loudly. He saw a few Cardinals and a group of finches hanging outback. A few swooped over the tree limbs and a few were near the grill on the patio, foraging the grass for any bugs they could find.

He tried to forget about what happened the day prior because it seemed bizarre and no one had believed him. He thought it had to have just been his imagination playing with him. Yet David had experienced the same strange phenomenon in the woods, so it must have been real.

Harold got up, got dressed and began his day, "Harold Breakfast is ready,' his mom shouted. He rushed out of his room, "Morning Momma, how're you this morning?", "I'm doing good baby, how are you?", "I'm fine, didn't sleep great but I'm alright," he replied. "What's for breakfast?", "We got eggs and some sausage links from the farm," Momma Tree said with her stomach rumbling. "Oh yum," Harold replied. He sat down at their small kitchen table that had a full view of the backyard and waited for her to bring his plate. "Thanks Momma", "no problem, babe," she said before placing both of their plates down on the table.

She sat down next to him after turning the stove off. "I got to work today honey, so try to get your homework done while I'm gone,", "okay Momma," Harold replied. Little did Momma Tree know, he had no ambition getting schoolwork done today. They finished eating breakfast and Harold was getting antsy, waiting for her to leave, so he could go fishing and take his mind away from the madness. "Alright sweetie I'm out of here, have a good day!", "you to momma, love you,", "love you to baby," Momma tree replied. She dashed out the door and went to work.

"Finally, now I can go fishing!" Harold was enthused; he grabbed his pole, slammed his feet into his boots and walked out the back door. There was a small pond in the woods behind his house that had a good amount of small mouth bass for him to fish. He walked into the woods, looking up at the birds singing. He whistled at them hoping to get them to sing the same tune back.

After a short hike, he finally made his way to the pond. He grabbed his pole and opened a small can of worms. He took his hook and attached the worm to it. Harold took a deep breath, lifted his head back and looked at the treetop. The sun shone and the leaves flew with the wind. He almost forgot about the insane week he had just had, until a crow started making noise. *Caw...Caw*, chills filled his spine and his eyes opened as wide as they could. He brushed it off and focused on fishing, he started jigging the worm on the pond floor, hoping to trigger the fish around it.

"Fish on! fish on!" He slung his pole over his shoulder hoping to set the hook and started reeling in. As he reeled the fish in, it had felt heavier than any fish he had caught in the pond yet. He couldn't believe how heavy it felt. Harold started to see the fish bubble on the surface and flap its tail when suddenly a bald eagle came out of nowhere and dove towards the fish. "Holy Moly," his fishing rod flung out of his hand, the bird swooped down and grabbed the fish, Harold tripped over his foot falling backwards.

He watched the bird take his fish away as his heart kept pounding, he smiled from ear to ear with amazement. "I have never seen a bald eagle so close, oh my god, that… was…incredible!" He said as he began standing up.

He grabbed his fishing pole, shook off the jitters and put a new worm on his hook, waiting to see if it would happen again. As he cast out his line the crow continued, *Caw…Caw,* it kept reminding him of yesterday and making him angry. Harold shrugged it off and again focused on fishing. After a few minutes, he had no bites and began reeling in his worm.

Halfway into reeling in his rod he felt a slight tug, as if the hook had caught something on the bottom of the pond. Harold raised an eyebrow but thought nothing of it and reeled it in while he looked up at the crow. As he looked down, he dropped his fishing pole, stunned, "h..h…h..how is that…even?...what…I…I… don't understand how?" The headless crow from the day before was on the end of his hook, saturated and decaying. He started to freak out and look around thinking, "Is someone messing with me?" He panicked, cutting the line to his fishing rod and running home.

He began sprinting as his house came into view, but the crow above him followed him and kept cawing exaggeratedly. "Leave me alone!" Harold shouted at the crow, but the crow kept following him, flying just above his head. *Caw…Caw,* Harold threw his fishing pole down on the ground of his backyard and opened the backdoor. He slammed it shut, locked it and fell to the floor hyperventilating. It was at this moment that he had finally accepted that everything he witnessed was true, he needed to find out how it could even be possible. "Why is this happening to me? what did I do to deserve this…the guys will never believe me…god what do I do!" he said, crying so hard that snot ran from his nose.

Harold sat there for a good half an hour then gathered his thoughts and got up. He went to his bedroom, sat at his desk and grabbed the homework from his backpack. As he began to try to distract himself, the crow that had been following him. It slammed into his bedroom window, Harold jumped up, shut the blinds and acted like it never happened because he was terrified.

Harold kept trying to do his homework, but his legs kept moving frantically and he just couldn't focus. He let out a loud sigh, "I can't do this right now," he got up and went over to the telephone. Harold called Evan's house to see if he was free, "hello?", "Hi, this is Harold, is Evan home?", "yes he is one second…hey Harold what's up?", "hey bro do you want to come over for a bit and play Atari?", "Sure let me ask real quick," Evan proceeded to ask his adoptive parents. "She said I could,", "awesome, see you soon," Harold replied. He hung up the phone and sat back down. He felt calm knowing he wouldn't be alone.

Evan lived on the other side of the road behind the Dingy Diner, so it only took him a few minutes to get there. *Knock…Knock,* Harold opened the door, "hey bro,", "hey Harold," Evan said. He stepped inside and felt a weird aura in the air, "where's your mom?", "she's at work until seven,", "oh okay…you okay man? you look anxious," Evan said. Harold wanted to tell him the truth that indeed he was not okay, but instead he bit his tongue. "Yeah bro…I'm okay, let's go play some games," the boys sat on Harold's bed, grabbed the Atari controllers and proceeded to play.

They began to play Combat and see who could win best out of five games. "Boom!" got you man," Evan said, winning round one. "I'll get you next round, watch out," Harold replied, nudging Evans shoulder. The boys finished playing and Evan won four out of five games. "I dominated you man, get good," Evan said jokingly. "Yeah, you got me this time bro," Harold replied.

Harold was happy that Evan decided to come over because it helped him stay calm and poise. "Hey, mom said I had to be back by five. It's four fifty-three, so I'm going to head out," Evan said. "Okay bro, I'll see you at school Monday. Have a good rest of your night bro and don't forget I'm going to beat your butt next time", "ha-ha you wish," Evan replied before he walked out the front door.

Harold shut the door behind him. He opened the fridge and made himself a bowl of cereal. "Oh, crap I forgot to finish my homework…oh well I'll do it after," He turned on the television and watched a show while he ate. He forgot to look outside to see if the crow that slammed into his window was dead or if it flew away.

As he finished eating, he opened the back door, looked around and saw nothing, so he shut the door. Harold walked back into his room, opened the blinds and saw faint blood stains on the outer glass. He grabbed the glass cleaner from under the kitchen sink and went outside to clean the window. As Harold came back inside Momma Tree had just pulled into the driveway.

She walked inside, exhausted from her day, turned around and Harold lunged at her, hugging her with all his might. "Hey babe are you okay?", "Yes Momma, I'm just happy you're home, I missed you," He replied. "Aww, honeybun, I missed you too. Did you get your homework done?" She spoke. Harold had completely forgotten about it but figured he would just lie so she didn't get angry. "Yes, Momma all done,", "good job honeybun," she smiled at him and kissed his forehead.

On the other side of town, Noah and Charleston were hanging out playing catch with a baseball in the road. "Hey bro, don't you think It's weird what happened to David yesterday?" Charleston said while throwing the ball to Noah. "Yeah, it was weird dude, but like come on he sounded insane!", "I know, but what if it was real and Harold found that crow as well," Charleston said. "Yea…ok…a headless crow that fell from the sky and lost its head somehow? I mean come on Charleston, you can't be that dumb and believe that story." Noah replied. Charleston shut his mouth and kept passing the baseball, he knew Noah wasn't going to believe them.

"Noah time to get ready for bed," his mother hollered. "Okay mom, be right there," he turned to Charleston and waved goodbye. Charleston started

to walk back to his house, muddled. "They have to
be telling the truth," He whispered to himself.

The next day began; it was a beautiful Sunday
morning with fog hovering over the grass.
Charleston woke up and decided to try to call
everyone to see if they wanted to hangout. All the
boy's parents agreed that it would be okay for them
to hangout for the day. They decided to meet
outside of the Diner just in front of Harold and
Evans' house. "Yoo," Noah said to Harold and Evan
who had already arrived. Shortly after Charleston
and David showed up and everyone began to chat.

"What did you want to do today Charleston?"
Evan asked. "I don't know man, I just wanted to see
if you all wanted to hangout," Charleston replied.
The boys all looked at each other to see if anyone
had any ideas. Harold spoke up, "we could go
hangout at the fishing hole behind my house for a
bit?", "ugh, fishing? I don't know how to fish! I
also don't like bugs. I hate mosquitos and they are
everywhere right now," Noah groaned. "Come on
Noah, stop being a baby," Charleston said, before
laughing at him and grabbing his shoulder. They
started walking over to the woods just beyond
Harold's house.

Harold almost forgot about the crow that he left near the edge of the pond, he was kind of scared to see if it was still there. He also didn't want to tell the boys everything that happened, just in case it somehow disappeared again. "Did Harold tell you guys that I whooped his butt on Atari yesterday?" Evan said, grinning. "Well, that's not saying much, I always beat him," Noah replied. "Yeah, yeah, you guys are better than me at video games, but I'm better at fishing. One second, I'm going to grab my pole," Harold said.

The boys waited for Harold at the beginning of the path. They began chasing each other around, throwing handfuls of grass at each other. Harold grabbed his fishing pole, running back over to his friends, they proceeded to walk into the woods. "Hey David, did you have any more weird experiences?" Charleston whispered to him. David just shook his head and kept walking, Charleston couldn't help but notice, David was being very quiet compared to normal.

As they neared the pond Harold began to sweat, becoming clammy and nervous, this might finally be the moment the boys all came together and witnessed what he had seen. They kept laughing and chatting as they had just arrived at the pond. "If I get a hundred mosquito bites and I'm itching all night, I'm blaming you Harold," Noah retorted. "Ha-ha okay man, I'll take the blame," Harold looked down and saw the soggy headless crow on the edge of the pond still.

He waited to see if anyone else would notice the crow, until Noah accidentally stepped on it. Noah looked down, he felt as though he had stepped on a sponge and screamed. "Ahhhh! Oh my god! it's got no head!" all the other boys gasped and looked at the crow. "I told you guys, but you didn't believe me,", "Now you finally see it! I was fishing yesterday, it grabbed my hook and scared the crap out of me when I reeled it in," Harold said.

Charleston couldn't believe his eyes, "Noah, you were wrong," he said. "I…I…I'm not wrong! These two are crazy! they are making stuff up," Noah shouted. Harold grabbed him with both arms, "I'm not making this up man, this is real,", "it can't be real! guys, Harold probably found a dead crow and cut its head off to try and convince us!" Noah replied. Charleston and Evan looked at each other skeptically.

"How could this even happen? is this the same crow from behind the school?" Evan said. "I think so, I don't know for sure because that one wasn't there anymore, but it could be," Harold said. Noah kept hyperventilating and losing his mind. "Get off me," He pushed Harold away and he started running back home.

The boys all shouted "Noah where are you going?", "Noah, come back!" then Evan said, "let him run…just…let him go," as he bent down to observe the crow. "I don't know how the crow got here guys, I just know that there is something weird going on," Harold said, letting out a sigh. "Well, we can't do anything about it now, but we believe you Harold. I'm sorry for doubting you before," Evan said, "yea I'm sorry," Charleston added. The boys all started walking back down the path, deciding to go back to their homes and sleep it off.

"Alright well I'll see you guys tomorrow, thanks for finally believing me," Harold said. He gave the guys a group hug and he walked back inside of his home. David, Evan and Charleston all walked to the diner. They saw Noah in his front yard crying, "do we go over or no?", "Don't bother. Go home let him figure it out and sleep on it," Evan said. The three of them all hugged again and went their separate ways.

As David was walking home with his head down, heavy footed, Ms. Jackson was outside weeding her garden. She couldn't help but notice he was kind of glum. "Hey David, honey are you okay?" she said. David looked over at her and replied, "I'm fine," and he kept walking back home. She thought it weird, but also not unordinary since he was always kind of sad anyway.

David got home and Josie tried to talk to him, but he went into his bedroom, closed the door and went to bed. "Is he okay?" Josie said to their mom, "I don't know sweetie, I'll go check," his mother knocked on his door. "David, are you okay?" she got no reply, "can I come in?" still no reply. She tried to go into his room, but it was locked and figured she would give him his space and leave him alone.

As Noah kept trying to stay asleep throughout the night, he continuously had flashbacks and horrors of the crow. He woke up pouring sweat from head to toe and freaking out every thirty minutes. He kept Thinking to himself, "I don't know what to believe anymore, god…what…how," Noah struggled for the remainder of the night. The sun slowly began to rise, he would have to go to school shortly, even though he was distraught, he got up and got ready.

4

DISCOVERY

Elvingdale wasn't a very big town nor was it a very popular town for tourists. In fact, it was rather boring, the only reason tourists would even think about visiting was because of the mall. The Diner was a staple for food in the entire state, but it never received very much advertisement. They had waffles with homemade butter and maple syrup that would knock the socks off anyone who loved a sugary explosion of flavor. The town had a big, beautiful forest surrounding it on all sides that had flows of streams, ponds and lots of wildlife.

Most days the town remained unbothered and gloomy from how quiet it could get. It had a past of hard work, blood, sweat and tears. The forest contained very thick brush that was hard to navigate through. Once you entered the woods, you could barely see outside of it.

The school day had started, and the boys continued to act as if nothing happened. Perhaps it was best they decided to avoid talking about the traumatic event. Noah was clearly distraught, he was not himself, but the other boys never brought it up. They focused on their schoolwork instead. Josie and Emma kept thinking about how quiet they all were. None of them seemed like themselves, including David.

As the day progressed the kids kept running rampant in thought, trying to figure out their next step. "Hey Noah are you okay?" Josie asked. She could clearly see something was disturbing him all day and he was not acting himself in the least bit. "Uh…umm…yes I'm fine Josie, how are you?" he replied. "I'm fine thank you for asking, if you need to talk at all about anything let me know," Josie said. She walked off and left the room as class came to an end.

Harold was itching to talk to Noah, but he didn't want to rush things, even though Harold was also struggling to understand what was going on. David was fast asleep at his desk, snoring as loud as the wind crackling against the trees outside. Harold poked David on the head, "hey bro it's time to go home," David slowly woke up, groggy and disgruntled. "Yep, okay mom, thank you," he replied. Harold looked at him with a confused look, laughed then walked off into the hallway.

Charleston and Noah gathered near the lockers and began to chat about the previous events. When Harold got close, they went quiet. "Hey guys what're you talking about?" Harold said, "Nothing dude, nothing," Noah replied. "Okay, well we got to talk about what happened at some point, so let me know when is good for you,", "yea man, no problem" Noah said. Harold continued down the hall until he reached the front door to head outside.

Harold walked past the girls and overheard them talking. "Hey Emma!", "Hey Josie," Emma replied, smiling. "Do you want to hang out again and maybe walk around town?" Josie asked. "Sure! Let me stop by home and drop off my stuff,", "okie dokie," Josie said before walking off.

"Hey Harold," Josie waved. He turned around and replied, "Hey Josie, what's up?", "What happened yesterday? you guys are all very quiet today and acting off?" She replied. He wanted to tell her but felt like it wasn't the right time. Harold thought that she would never believe him anyway. "Oh nothing, just boy stuff," Harold said. Josie could tell he was hiding something but refused to pry. "Ha-ha okay Harold, have a good night!", "yeah…you to Josie," he then walked away and continued home.

Josie got to her house and walked inside to see her parents watching tv. "Hi honey, how was school?", "it was good, a bit boring but good!", "that's good, where is David?", "I don't know, I think he's coming," She responded. Josie didn't want to rat him out and tell his parents that he was sleeping in class. Meanwhile David was still in the classroom.

He was looking off in the distance at the chalk board, having visualizations of the crow missing its head. He kept twitching and rubbing his eyes but remained seeing the gruesome scene repetitively. "David, are you okay?" Ms. Jackson asked, "yea I'm fine," he grabbed his backpack, stood up and tripped over his desk. "Have a good day, bye," he said, hurrying out of the door. Ms. Jackson thought nothing of it because David fell asleep in class quite often and it was a normal occurrence.

David avoided Noah and Charleston in the hallway. He walked outside, deciding to take a right and follow the fence to the wood line. Josie was in the house grabbing some food when she saw him out of the window and wondered where he could be going. "Hey, I'm going to hang out with Emma, I'll be back soon," Josie said. "Okay honey," Josie dashed out the doorway with her muffin in hand and followed David without him noticing.

David started to walk into the wood line and saw the stream of water where he had the first encounter. He put his backpack down and started to walk down the hill. Hoping that maybe he could better understand what was going on. Josie followed him down the trail, hiding behind trees every now and then to avoid detection. He made it to the water and sat down.

Looking to his left, he saw normal woods, thick bushes and tall trees, nothing unusual. He then looked to his right, he saw the same thick bushes and taller trees, but then he noticed that the stream had almost disappeared into the thicket. It looked like an entrance to a part of the woods he had never seen before. David got up, dusted all the leaves off his bottom and started walking to the right, following the stream.

The stream was as low as it ever got but had about a three-foot high-water mark. Josie stayed back, "what is he even doing? he looks like he is searching for something?" she said to herself. He finally made it to the edge of the thicket. "How do I even get through this? Does this contain the answers we are looking for? what could even be back here since you can't even walk there?" He thought endlessly.

David hopped down in the stream since he couldn't walk anywhere through the thicket. He got low, passing under the roots and bushes that hung over the stream. He started to make his way down inside a tunnel, following the stream bed. Josie quickly ran to the edge of the thicket and waited for him to get far enough to hop in and follow him. David kept walking with his legs getting soaked in the water sloshing around. "How far does this go?" he said out loud. He seemed to be under vines and bush for about fifty feet now, but he could see an opening coming up. David made it to the end of the tunnel and his jaw dropped.

"Oh…my…god," he came to an entanglement of trees that twisted and bent every direction. Surrounding it was a fortress of bushes and vines that circled the trees all the way around. He stood in the stream shocked to see a tall door made of woven vines and bark. "I found it, this must be what's causing all these weird things to happen. It almost looks like a castle of some sort," he said to himself.

Josie hopped down into the stream and started to follow him down the tunnel. David was heading back and locked eyes with her, she smiled. "Josie, are you following me?" She didn't reply, she just sort of grinned and giggled. "Go back it's not safe!" He trudged towards her as she backed up. "Okay

David I'm leaving, but why isn't it safe? what did you see?" she said. "Oh…nothing…just it isn't safe," he replied, trying to keep it a secret. Josie knew something was up at that time but again decided to remain silent. She was determined that she would come back to this tunnel and find out what he saw.

They both made it back up the hill and didn't talk about anything. David grabbed his backpack and walked home while Josie stood there for a second at the tree line. She wondered what time she should come back.

Josie went over to Emma's house next door. She knocked on her door; Emma opened the door and hugged her. "Hey girl! are you ready to go on a walk?" Josie said, "Heck yes, let's go!" Emma shut the door behind her. The girls held hands skipping down the road.

They looked over and saw Ms. Jackson arrived home and waved to her. "Josie, did Evan ever come up to you yet?" Emma asked, "sort of but not as much as I want him to!" she chuckled. The girls continued to walk around the town. "Oh my god the food smells so good at the diner right now," Josie raved. "Girl, you're telling me," The smell of freshly cooked bacon filled the air. Both girls wanted to go grab some food but decided not to and just kept walking.

"The boys were acting really weird today huh?" Josie stated. "Oh my god they were so weird…well I mean, like, they were acting normal instead of being weird like normal ha-ha," Emma replied. "Yea I think something is going on that they are not telling us," Josie said. "Like what?", "I'm not sure, but I think we can find out tonight.", "What do you mean?" Emma replied. "I'll tell you later, let's just keep walking" Josie said before kissing Emma's hand and running down the road, racing Emma.

"Noah has such a big house. I mean my house is close in size, but they have so much stonework and it just looks so beautiful.:" Emma said. "I know, I always get jealous when I pass his house, his dad is never home much though," Josie mentioned. "Yeah, I wish my stepdad wasn't home so much! ha-ha" Emma giggled. They started to make their way around the bend, back towards the school.

"Can we stop by my dad really quick?" Emma asked shyly, "of course we can!" Josie replied. The girls walked into the graveyard; Emma sat down next to her dad's headstone and began to talk to him. "Hi daddy I hope you are having a good day, I won't take too much of your time, but I love you very much. I'm hanging out with Josie, and we are having a lot of fun. I'll talk to you later, bye daddy." Emma prayed, stood up and kissed the side of his headstone. Josie couldn't help but shed a tear, thinking about how beautiful of a person Emma is and how much she loved her dad.

"Alright Josie so what is it you said earlier about finding out what the boys are up to tonight?" Emma mentioned. "Oh right! follow me," Josie replied before grabbing Emma's hand. The girls began to make their way to the tree line and Josie filled Emma in. "I followed David earlier and he walked down here in the woods into the stream. He saw something but wouldn't tell me what he saw. I figured we could go check it out before it gets dark out," Josie said. "Okay, that sounds good," Emma replied.

They walked down the hill and came to the same thicket that David was at earlier. "How do we get around it?" Emma asked. "We don't really get around it. I think the only way is to hop into the stream and go under the vines," Josie replied. She hopped into the stream and left her arm out for Emma to grab. Emma joined her and made a big splash as she hit the water. "Alright, now we just go under these bushes and vines," Josie said. "I'm scared Josie," Emma mumbled. "It's okay Emma,

I'm here," Josie grabbed her hand and held her closely.

The girls waded down the stream until they saw the opening on the other side. "We're almost there Emma,", "good because this tunnel is spooky," Emma replied. They got to the end of the tunnel and saw the bright sun setting beyond the trees, they gasped out of amazement. "What is this place?", "oh my god," Emma said. "I don't know, I knew something was up when I saw David's face after coming down here," Josie replied.

They stood up, standing in the stream. Vines and thorn bushes surrounded both edges of the stream. "It looks like those vines and bark are some sort of door or something," Josie said eagerly. "I think so," Emma replied. "Let's see if we can open it really quick," Josie began to push on the bark, it stood firm.

"Rrrrggh it won't budge", "did you try to pull it? Emma said. Josie began to pull on the vine cluster, holding the Bark in place. "Still nothing, I don't know, Emma it won't move," Josie said, disheveled. "Okay well at least we know it's here, this is really weird though because it doesn't look man made," Emma replied. Josie stood back a bit, "do you see those trees? They are pine trees, but unlike normal pine trees, these ones are all crooked and form strange loops," she said. "Yeah, that's interesting," Emma replied.

The girls began to gather their thoughts, figuring out what this could be and how it relates to the boys being weird today at school. "Alright well we clearly can't get in so let's head back," Emma said. "Okay Emma, let's go," the girls made their way back through the tunnel, up the hill and back to Emma's house. "We need to figure this out. Thank you for showing me, Josie, that place looked so cool," Emma gushed, "No problem, Emma! I hope you have a good night, I'll see you tomorrow," Josie replied. She shut the door and walked back to the road.

Josie couldn't help but ask herself, "why did David say it wasn't safe? what did he mean by that?" She wanted to ask him so badly but decided to wait until tomorrow. She walked into her house and grabbed a glass of water. "Hi honey, did you have fun with Emma?", "yes I did thank you," Josie smiled. "Well get some rest, it's getting late,", "will do, have a good night," She replied. Josie ran up the stairs to her room and got ready for bed.

5

Confrontation

The day had begun and the sound of rainfall took over the neighborhood. Emma was fast asleep, at peace and had no plans on waking up anytime soon. The rain was beading from her windows in a melodic manor that left her dazed. "Ugh…not yet," she said as she rubbed her eyes and stretched her legs. Emma only had about five more minutes until she had to get up for school or she would be late. She was going to soak and cherish these last couple minutes.

"Okay," she said, "I think I'm ready to finally get up," she went downstairs with her pajamas on and made a glass of orange juice. "Good morning, Mom,", "Good morning honey, did you sleep okay?", "yes, the rain is relaxing. I've been struggling to stay awake," they both smiled and enjoyed their breakfast. Emma made her way back upstairs, grabbed her schoolbag and filled it with her finished homework from the weekend.

Josie was over at her house doing the same thing. She was still curious what David knew about the place they had just discovered, but she waited to ask him since he was groggy and barely able to stand. "Have a good day at school you two!", "you to mom!" David replied. Josie and David started walking over to school with their rain boots on and raincoats over their backpacks braving the weather. Even though it was a short walk, it was raining so hard they were bound to be drenched before they got there.

They made it to school early while the other kids all took the bus. "David give me your coat, I'll hang it up", "okay. Here," David said as he gave it to Josie. She looked back at him and said, "by the way…what is that place I followed you to? I brought Emma afterwards and we couldn't figure out what it was," She mentioned. "You did what? Why would you go back," he replied angrily.

Josie was surprised by his emotion. She didn't notice anything scary or dangerous about the place, so she was perplexed. "Yea…why are you so angry? it wasn't even dangerous,", "we don't know what that place is, but we think it's linked to a bunch of strange things that keep happening. I'll talk about it later at home, don't go back again, okay?" David answered. "Okay I'll stay away," Josie replied, agreeing with him.

The kids all had weary bouts in their eyes while they tried to focus on school. Ms. Jackson could tell something was very different today, she sensed a disturbance in the air that carried through most of her classroom. She wondered if it could be because of the weather outside. The rain was continuous and heavy. "Alright class welcome in I hope you all are doing well; you all did good last week. I think it's time we switch over to literacy for the semester," Ms. Jackson noted.

Ms. Jackson carried on with her practice, but getting the students to engage wasn't working. "Hey Harold," David said, "I saw things in the woods, we need to go where I went and figure out what's going on,", "okay, that's a great idea, try to ask the other guys quickly when Ms. Jackson isn't looking. Tell them to meet us in the hall after class," Harold replied. David started asking Evan, Charleston, and Noah if they would be able to meet them in the hallway after class to discuss plans. All the boys nodded and proceeded to focus on their schoolwork.

The bell had rung and class had ended. "Have a good night, everyone, remember your homework is due in three days. Study hard and take this book to help you with the answers." Ms. Jackson handed each student a pamphlet with an English study book that covered the basics of literacy and grammar. Josie and Emma were both chatting at the end of the line, "did you find anything out from David?" Emma asked. "No, he freaked out at me and told me to stay away from the area, something is definitely going on. We need to find out what they are up to," Josie commented. "Yeah, we should totally keep an eye on them from now on," Emma replied.

All the students left the classroom for the end of the day and the boys gathered up next to Harold's locker. Noah gave Harold knuckles. Evan, Charleston and David all huddled closely waiting for Harold to discuss the plans of action.

"Firstly, hey guys, I hope you guys feel okay and slept last night," Harold said. The guys all looked away and seemed rather sickly. "What are we doing here? Please tell me we are not going in the woods," Noah exclaimed. "Don't be so scared," Charleston muttered, "guys focus, I saw something crazy in the woods, and we have to find out what it was," David added. "Okay man, damn David, I've never seen you this anxious before." Noah said. "Yeah, well my sister followed me and is asking questions," He responded. The guys all looked at each other with unease and then made eye contact with Josie and Emma.

The girls happened to be hanging out at Josie's locker spying on them. Josie waved at the boys and smiled; she had suspicion that David just told them what she was up to. "Okay well if she knows something is up then we need to be more careful. In case it is dangerous we must keep them safe," the boys all nodded in agreement. "I think we should all try to sneak out tonight and make our way back down to the woods. Let's figure out once and for all what that place is and why it exists," Harold said. Emma happened to be walking by at the perfect time to gather information on their plan when she went to the water fountain to get a drink. She then walked back to Josie and left school together.

The boys were still gathered, and Ms. Jackson had overheard them talking, it sparked curiosity in her veins. "How are we supposed to sneak out? like my dad stays up late I can't sneak by him man," Noah said. "Ask him if you can spend the night at my house," Harold replied. Noah let out a sigh and bit his lip, "fine, I'll try,", "anybody else worried about sneaking out?" No one made a noise. "Okay it looks like a plan then, let's meet up at the tree line at ten pm. Make sure to bring flashlights and bring boots. I'm going to bring my mom's machete just in case." The boys all agreed, broke their huddle and proceeded to walk home.

Noah was freaking out the whole time walking home nervous. What if they got attacked in the woods by demons or a big foot lived in those vines and they would get eaten by him. He was pouring sweat as he walked in the door. He decided to go take a shower to cool down before his dad got home from work. Noah got done showering and packed his bag with a flashlight, inhaler, gloves and a pocketknife for defense.

His dad got home and Noah asked, "hey pops how was work?", "It was good son, how was your day?", "It went well. I was wondering if I could spend the night at Harolds? he wanted my help with homework," Noah claimed. "Yeah, that sounds fine. Make sure you bring your toothbrush,". "Of course, thank you," Noah hugged his dad, ran upstairs and put his toothbrush in his bag. He went back downstairs, left his house and went across the street to Harolds.

The day became evening and Josie was hanging out with Emma at her house, about to have dinner with her mother and stepdad. The girls spent hours talking about the boy's plans and what they should do.

Finally, dinner was served with steak and broccoli, the girls devoured the food. They requested to be excused from the table to go work on homework together. "Hey mom, can Josie spend the night actually?", "sure honey," she replied. Josie and Emma hung out in Emma's room for an hour or two thinking of what to bring with them.

A couple houses over Noah was hanging out at Harolds and playing video games waiting for nightfall. "Hey man, do you think we will find anything tonight? like I was thinking, what if this is where bigfoot lives and we intrude in his swamp and he kills us?" Noah said, nervously. "Bro what? Big foot doesn't exist," Harold snickered. "Yea well a headless crow that had a head before it flew into a magical wall or something sounds fake to," Noah replied. Noah was clearly shaken up about everything and was struggling to process every bit of information. "I guess you are right Noah, but we still have to find out what's going on because I don't think anybody else will," Harold said. Noah looked at Harold and agreed with tired eyes.

The time was nine pm, Charleston and Evan had already been fully packed ready to go on the adventure of a lifetime. Emma was finishing packing her favorite stuffed elephant that her dad gave her before he passed. It kept her safe and helped her stay calm. "Did your dad give you that? It's cute. I like it," Josie said. "Yes, he did, he bought it for me when we went to New York on vacation," Emma replied. Josie could tell Emma was anxious but wanting to go, so she decided to hug her very tightly. "I know you miss your dad still, but he will keep us safe tonight, don't worry" Josie mentioned. "Thank you, I know he will" Emma said while grabbing Josie tightly and smiling.

They finished packing their bags with flashlights and Emma grabbed some pepper spray from her mom's purse. The time had finally come, the girls watched from Emma's window looking out at the tree line. "Oh, look it's Evan and Charleston," Emma said. They appeared to be the first ones there and ready to go. Shortly after she saw David creeping out the back door and joining them. Harold and Noah were last but not too far behind.

Ms. Jackson was doing her final set of house chores, cleaning the counter talking to her kitty Snuggles. When she saw all the boys by the tree line. "Oh gosh it's late, what could they even be doing?" she said. Ms. Jackson couldn't help but think how she herself had never been into those parts of the woods, maybe the kids were in danger. She decided to go get dressed and look for a flashlight. Ms. Jackson waited for them to enter the woods before she left her house to follow them.

Emma and Josie decided to meet with the boys instead of following them because they felt safer. "Alright boys let's do this, no matter what happens we will get to the bottom of this," Harold declared. Evan appeared ready as a gladiator and asked Harold, "Can I carry the machete and lead the way?", "Of course you can!" Harold didn't hesitate to respond because he knew he didn't want to go first. The boys gathered and were ready to head into the woods, but they noticed something off in the distance.

"Look!" Evan nudged David's shoulder, "is that who I think it is?", "Oh crud," David sighed. The girls were walking towards them, "here we go," Josie said to Emma. "What are you guys doing here?" David shouted. "Shush, you're going to wake them," Josie responded. "It doesn't matter why they are here, but they decided to join us, it won't change a thing. We are still going to figure out what this place is," Harold said, making sure they all agreed.

Evan had a huge smile on his face looking at Josie, she couldn't help but smile back. "Glad you girls are joining us, I'm going to lead the way, so stay back with the other guys," Evan insisted. They began to walk into the woods and turned their flashlights on. They heard crows cawing, Harold shined his light up at a tree and saw dozens of crows all hanging out on tree branches. "Do we turn back? I don't know guys this feels wrong," Noah panicked. "Come on, stop being such a baby we got this," Charleston replied. Evan led the way watching his foot placement because it was hard to see anything. The hill was steep enough to cause injury if you were not careful.

As they edged closer to the stream and entranceway the ground started to tremble and the crows all flew in front of them. The crows landed in the water, viciously cawing and throwing themselves around. The girls let out a soft scream and hid behind the boys while they stood in silence and fear.

Ms. Jackson had made her way out of the door and heard the scream in the distance. She thought the worst, so she started bolting towards them. Evan jumped down in the water and started swatting at the crows with the machete and they all flew away. He let out his hand, "here Harold, come on," Harold grabbed his hand and jumped in the water. Evan helped everyone else down into the water. He then went back to the front of the line and started to travel into the tunnel of vines that led them to the hidden forest.

Emma and Josie were holding hands the whole way because the mud under their feet kept shaking, they heard strange noises as they got closer to the end of the tunnel. Ms. Jackson finally made her way into the woods and went down the hill where she last saw the kids go. She didn't see a single soul, but she saw the crows muttering in the trees. She didn't know what to do but the screaming had stopped. She decided to go back home and wait for them to come back out of the woods to make sure they were okay.

The kids finally reached the entrance of the fortress, they all sat in awe as the vines moved about and the trees kept bending, shaking and twisting. "I don't believe what I'm seeing," Evan said. "What is this place?" Noah asked. "We don't know but we are here to find out," David replied. They looked at the entrance and hidden on a rock, under the vines it read, *Castle of Pine*.

Harold looked at it for a second. He then looked back at the vines which seemed to be alive. "This place is called the Castle of Pine," he said to everyone. "It has the name of it on this rock, which I believe is where the entrance is," Harold stated.

Evan walked over to Harold, "Stand back man," Evan took the machete out of the sheath and started hacking at the vines as hard as he could. Every time he broke a vine it would suddenly regrow and fortify. "Huh, that's weird," he said. Harold told him, "Stop…that's clearly not going to work," and he began to wonder if they could even get inside.

Suddenly everyone heard the caws of hundreds of crows barreling towards them through the tunnel. They moved back from the entrance and the vines opened just enough to let the crows in. As the vines opened, the crows flew by and the smell of death wreaked the air. The smell became piercing and overwhelming until finally all the crows went in, causing the vines to close back up. "What in the hell was that? We need to leave now," Noah screamed, "no!" Harold replied. Harold thought he understood what had just happened, "don't you guys see the Crows made noises and vibrations that the vines accepted and allowed them to enter," everyone looked at him like he was crazy. All they saw was a murder of crows flying into what appeared to be a trap.

Harold wanted to try something, he began to caw like the crows and vines started to open slowly. As he kept cawing, the vines realized he was an imposter and a voice screamed at them, "run!"

Emma fell into the stream and everyone else fell back on their butt. The girls started screaming and crying, "go let's go now!" The boys were scared for their lives, they all hurried back through the tunnel on all fours as fast as they could.

The voice began laughing at them in a creepy dark tone that echoed throughout the tunnel. They all got to the end, "Hurry!" Noah yelled. Evan grabbed everyone's hand to get them out of the stream, and they scurried up the hill. More crows sat in the trees cawing at them the entire way, as if they were mocking them and laughing at how scared they were. Finally, everyone made it to the top of the hill, out of the trees and they all collapsed on the grass, breathing heavily.

Ms. Jackson was drinking tea and reading a book while waiting. She took a glance, looking out of the window again and saw all the kids sitting on the ground looking like they just saw a ghost. She felt relieved and at least knew they were okay, so she decided to go to bed and talk about it tomorrow at school.

"I think we're going to go back to my house" Emma insisted, she stood up and grabbed Josie's hand. "Okay, we should all hurry back home, we will talk more tomorrow," Harold replied. "Not cool man, not cool at all," Noah complained following Harold back to his house. The other boys all went back to their homes and snuck their way to bed.

Emma and Josie went back into Emma's room and hugged each other for comfort. Emma took her elephant out of her bag, kissed it and said, "thank you for keeping me safe daddy." The girls cuddled under the blankets out of fear and went to sleep.

6

CURIOSITY

All the children woke up feeling crummy. They did not know what mysteries they just uncovered and felt lucky to be unscathed. The kids started to get ready for school but were afraid of even walking outside knowing the potential dangers that lie in the woods.

The bus continued around the small town, picking up each child for school. As each one of them boarded the bus, they kept quiet and wouldn't even look at each other. "Okay kids have a great day at school and I'll see you later," the bus driver announced as he arrived in the lot.

Charleston was in the back seat pondering what Harold said. He was processing how the sounds could potentially be the key to opening the obstruction of vines and tree limbs. Noah noticed Charleston deep in thought. "Hey dude, you, okay? we are at school let's go," Charleston jumped and replied, "Yeah I'm fine man, I'm fine," they then got off the bus and hurried to class.

"Good morning class, I hope you all had a good weekend and got some of your homework done. Remember this week we have another test," Ms. Jackson mentioned. She continued her lesson of the day. She wanted to ask the children whom she saw outside late at night what they were up to.

Class was about to come to an end, "Noah, Josie, Emma, Charleston, David, Evan, and Harold, can you please stay after class for a minute?" Ms. Jackson said. The kids all locked eyes with each other and their jaws dropped. All the other kids in the class were pointing fingers, muttering about. The bell rang, all the other kids left the classroom, and Ms. Jackson closed the door behind them.

"Children, I'm not trying to be nosey, but last night I saw you all leaving the woods and you looked frightened," The kids froze. "Ye…ye…yes, we saw a bear when we're playing a game," Emma replied hastily. "Oh my god! Are you guys, okay?" Ms. Jackson was stunned, "Yes, we are fine, we got a little too close and it scared us. Luckily it didn't chase us," Harold cleverly responded. "Okay kids well it's probably best not to go back into the woods anytime soon then." Ms. Jackson replied. Everyone responded at the same time, "Yes Ms. Jackson,", "Go ahead and leave, that's all I wanted to know. I'm glad you all are okay," She added.

Ms. Jackson was clearly hesitant and unsure whether they were telling the truth or not, but she had no choice but to believe them now. The kids dashed into the hallway and surrounded Harold's locker. "Guys, guys, what the heck just happened...she caught us?" Noah said in a frenzy. "Calm down bro, it's okay thanks to Emma and her quick thinking, she doesn't suspect a thing," Harold replied. Josie grabbed Emma and wrapped her arms around her, squeezing her "thank you, that was really smart," Josie said, smiling from ear to ear.

"What do we do now?" David asked, sweating from his forehead as if he had run a mile up a hill. "I'm not exactly sure, but if my theory is correct then we could find a way to open the entrance and figure out what is inside," Harold articulated. "Well, I think it's very clear that this is some sort of magical enchantment or something. Unworldly that no one has ever come across before," Evan said. All the other kids looked at him and didn't want to believe what he said to be true but felt the same.

"Magic?! there's no such thing, what are you guys talking…this can't be real," Noah started freaking out and losing his mind. "Noah…Noah! Calm down and breathe. We can't have you having an asthma attack right now…Breathe," Charleston said as he grabbed Noah's shoulders. "I'm sorry I

74

just…*Noah puffed his inhaler*…I can't believe we witnessed this," Noah said. "None of us can, but we will figure out what to do next. Let's try to all meet at the Diner later in about two hours," Harold declared. They all nodded in agreement and dispersed to their lockers before heading home. Everyone chose to walk home since it would be a time to reflect and think of any ideas.

Emma wanted to stop by her father's grave real fast before she got home and say a prayer to keep her and her friends safe, no matter what happens. She arrived at his grave, kneeled and interlocked her hands. "Daddy, I hope you are doing well wherever you are. My friends and I discovered some weird things in the woods the other day. I'm reaching out to you now to ask for your protection. Please help us stay safe and give us the strength to figure out what is going on. I love you very much, amen," She said before opening her eyes.

As she was about to get up a ladybug had landed on her nose, it looked at her for a few seconds before flying off. She whispered to herself, "this must be daddy reaching out," then smiled. She got back up and continued to walk home. The kids all got back to their houses and began to think of an excuse to be able to go to the diner with their friends.

Most of them told their parents they wanted to go study with friends for their test this week at the diner and were allowed to go. The only one who didn't have the same idea but decided he was going to sneak out was Harold. He lived very close to the diner, but he could easily go out the back door and sneak around the side of his house with ease. Before he left, he jotted down a map of the layout of the woods. The small pond where he found the dead bird, to the stream which the tunnel connected to. He folded the map, stuffed it in his pocket and continued out the door.

Ms. Jackson luckily didn't have to spend much time in the classroom once the day was over. She arrived at her house and got her house key to unlock her front door. Suddenly she heard a high pitch hissing noise in the bushes near her door, and it piqued her interest. Ms. Jackson decided to walk back down the steps and see what the noise could be. The bush startled and began to shake as she approached it. The hissing began to louden, and her heart started to race, "maybe I should go back inside," She blurted.

Right when she was about to walk inside, she looked down and saw a colony of rats flooding from the bush by the dozens. They were no ordinary rats but instead they had eyes missing and flesh rotting,

bubbles in their fur with feet limping. Ms. Jackson
let out a short scream, grabbed her purse on the
steps and quickly made her way inside. She started
yelling, "Snuggles! where are you baby?" searching
under the living room couch, scouring for him in a
craze.

She thought the worst and was hoping to God
that the rats didn't somehow get inside. For all she
knew there could be hundreds more of them and she
never saw anything like them before. She went
upstairs to her bedroom, "snuggles…honey…it's
mama," she called and bent over to look under the
bed. "Oh my, there you are baby! thank goodness,"
She was relieved.

Snuggles was sleeping, cozied up in his favorite
spot under the bed on a little blanket she put there
for him. Ms. Jackson grabbed him and held him
closely while she wiped a tear from her eye in
relief. Snuggles let out a big ole yawn that smelt
like tuna fish and chicken. She kissed him on the
forehead, petting his chin then let him return to his
napping session.

Ms. Jackson went downstairs and checked every
room for any signs of rats, looking at the bottom
corner of the walls for any holes or crevices. She
couldn't find a single sign that they made their way

inside, so she took a breather. "There was definitely something wrong with those rats, that was really strange," she mumbled. After she calmed down, she grabbed a coffee mug and poured herself some tea.

At this time the children had arrived at the diner to discuss their journey ahead. Josie arrived and saw Noah, Charleston, Emma, and Harold all sitting there in a booth. Emma waved at Josie to come over and sit down. "Hey where's David?" Harold asked, "I don't think he is going to come, he's been really shaken up over this," Josie replied. "Okay, well welcome! I got us all milkshakes, so grab whatever one you want, we have Vanilla, chocolate and strawberry ones," Harold said. "Thanks Harold," Josie grabbed herself a strawberry milkshake because that was her favorite flavor and sat down next to Emma.

Evan walked through the door shortly after and sat down. "Okay now that we all are here, well, at least all of us that are going to show up. It's time we go over a game plan and think of a strategy to uncover what's going on in the woods." Harold took out his map and plopped it on the table for everyone to see.

"Here is our town layout, we got the diner south and the mall just above us to the north. The woods are along the edge behind my house to the school, so it carries from the west to far north and ends once it reaches the other side of our school," Harold explained. He grabbed his pencil in his pocket and began to outline the woods.

"It's very clear to me that whatever this magic is, it's only powerful in the woods," He circled the section where they found the Castle of Pine. "How do you know that?" Noah asked. "Well, when that crow was flying and it looked like it hit an invisible wall before going into the woods, that seemed like a sign of passage," Harold replied. "Why would it stop the crow? especially if it's working with it?" Charleston asked. "I'm not sure, we know we can walk in those woods, and it doesn't stop us, but once we are inside bizarre things start happening around us," Harold said. "Maybe the crow is being controlled by something?" Emma said. Everyone looked at her and thought she might be onto something.

The kids all started to think that maybe whatever is in the woods behind those vines and limbs might be controlling all the wildlife around it. "If it could control crows to stop dead in their tracks and also make their heads come clean off… maybe…just maybe…it wants us in there to do the same to us?" Harold specified. Noah took a puff of his inhaler anxiously, "I don't like this,", "neither do I bro but maybe it's taunting us. That's why it showed us the crows and had them cawing at us. We are being played," Charleston replied.

They all began to get nervous, "what's our plan? what do we do," Josie asked. "I say we all gear up, bring flashlights, any weapons you can find and finally find out what is going on for real. We strike at night when it's the most powerful and we enter the forbidden zone, once and for all," Harold declared.

"Okay, but we can't get in? we tried," Evan reminded everyone. "I know but I think if I bring my guitar and play a song in a specific key, that it might unlock the doorway long enough for us to enter," Harold said. "Genius," Emma shouted. "What day and what time do you plan on doing this?" Charleston asked. "I say we strike tomorrow night and meet at the tree line again at dusk,", "what about Ms. Jackson, she saw us last time?" Josie mentioned. "Don't worry about it, if she does no big deal" Harold replied.

He finished his milkshake and put the map back in his pocket. Even though he drew the map, he barely needed it. They all said their goodbyes and walked out of the diner heading back home.

1

Cube of Faith

The clock struck 6:45 a.m. The sound of television static woke Harold. Startled, he rubbed his eyes and rushed his fingers through his hair to wake himself up. He got out of bed and let out a big yawn, stretching hard enough to almost reach the ceiling. He knew today was going to be no joke, but he also felt strong and ready after all the events that took place. He hopped in the shower, got dressed and went into the kitchen for breakfast with Momma Tree.

She had cooked up an array of eggs, pancakes, waffles and bacon, Harold's eyes lit up because his stomach was grumbling. "Morning Momma, I hope you slept well" Harold said. "You too baby, now eat up and get ready for school," she replied. "Yes Momma," he finished his breakfast and packed his schoolbag.

He glanced over and saw the small map of Elvingdale he had pinned up on the wall. "It's time…it's time to finally figure out what in the heck is going on in this town." Harold muttered before grabbing his schoolbag and walking back to the kitchen. "Bye Momma, have a good day now," he said, smiling. "Bye sweetie, tell Barb I said hi," she responded. "I will," Momma Tree smiled and kissed her son on the forehead, Harold slugged his boots on and made his way out the front door.

Down the road Ms. Jackson had been sleeping in after her chain of events the night before and had nightmares of wicked obscurities. She opened her right eye while still being nestled under the comforter, "Good morning Snuggles,", "meow." Snuggles replied. Ms. Jackson giggled and gave him plenty of belly tickles before getting up. Like any other morning without a thought in mind, she was ready to take on the day and whatever it may bring.

Ms. Jackson made her way downstairs and was barely awake, rubbing her eyes and gently yawning, then she stopped completely still. She could not believe what she was seeing and fear automatically took control of her entire body. She let out an enormously loud scream, her kitchen smelt of rancid meat. There were rats covering the entire floor inch by inch, the counter tops swarming with more rats and cereal boxes devoured into tiny shreds of cardboard.

She quickly took hold of the broomstick in the corner and began smashing and bashing with brute force on every rat in sight. Sounds of their little cries echoed as she annihilated them, "no ... .no…no…this is MY HOUSE!" she said, fuming. After about five minutes of swinging the broom like a baseball bat she needed to catch her breath. The remainder of the rats scurried their way back outside through a hole in the wall that they made themselves. She stopped and looked at the kitchen, seeing blood and tiny organs on the cabinets. Feeling defeated she couldn't help but fall down crying.

After letting her emotions out and taking the time to relax, she got herself up and reached for the phone. Ms. Jackson thought it would be a good idea to call an exterminator to seal the house from pests. After her call, she grabbed all the kitchen rags she could find and began to mop up the scene. Every swing of the rag caused a swooshing, debilitating feeling of disgust. Realizing how long it was going to take, she decided to call into work at the last minute. She let them know she won't be in today, making up the excuse of being sick.

The children all arrived at school, looking eager to get the day over with so that night fall may commence. Everyone sat in their chairs waiting for

Ms. Jackson to arrive, "huh she's not usually late?" Emma said. The other kids didn't seem to notice or really think about it considering tonight was the night they planned on finally getting into the Castle. Harold kept looking over at everyone thinking to himself. "I sure hope we are ready for this," as if he knew the horror that was lingering on the other side.

The principal soon walked into the classroom. He announced that Ms. Jackson would not be coming in today and that he would be subbing in for her.

The morning continued to drag for the kids, they were beyond ready to venture into the woods again. Josie stood up and walked to the back to sharpen her pencil, Evan came up behind her, "Hey Josie, how are you?" he gushed. "I'm doing okay…are you ready for later?" she replied. "Yes, I'm super ready, nervous, but ready." Evan said.

Josie smiled anxiously at him then went back to her chair. She had always fancied Evan but never knew how to engage with boys. He had confidence in him that protruded with anyone he talked to. Josie, on the other hand, lacked confidence and self-belief.

The bell had rung and the kids raced into the hallway. They made a circle around Harold, "Okay, tonight we find out what is plaguing our town. Tonight we must be stronger than before and be ready for anything. We have no idea what we will see or walk into once we open the passageway, so prepare yourselves now. Stick together and if anyone freaks out try and comfort them," Harold said.

Emma looked extremely scared and so did Josie. The boys seemed unfazed for the most part, other than David. He started to sweat heavily and felt like passing out. "How are you going to open the gate?" Charleston asked. "Like I said earlier, I think if I bring my guitar and play a song it might open the passage long enough for us to enter," Harold replied. "Okay but like how will we get out? Dude this is crazy, what if we get stuck?" Noah said frantically before puffing his inhaler. "As long as I still have my guitar, we should be able to reopen it without any problems. On the off chance we get stuck in there, we must remain calm and try to find a way out," Harold replied.

They all nodded back at him as reality finally hit. "I will see you at the tree line around dusk. Bring flashlights, food, water, and a weapon of some sort." Harold said before walking out of the school. On his walk home he constructed a strategy in his head, thinking about every possibility they could encounter. He knew they might not make it out, so he decided he would write a letter to his mother when he got home.

As Harold was walking past Ms. Jackson's house, he happened to see an exterminator there and whispered to himself, "huh, that's probably why she called out. I knew she wasn't sick." He shortly arrived at his house, walked through the door and put his boots on the mat before heading to his room. Harold grabbed a piece of paper and a pencil to begin writing his letter to Momma Tree.

> *'Dear momma, I hope you realize how much I love you. You are such a beautiful woman, with such a kind heart. You are the best cook I know and work so hard. If you are reading this letter, it's because I haven't returned home from the night before. Please do not worry because I promise to find my way back shortly. You will forever be the best mom a young man could ever have.*

Love, Harold'

He couldn't help but sob after writing this letter thinking this might be the last day ever seeing her. He folded the letter up, stuck it in an envelope and left it on his desk.

Down the road Ms. Jackson greeted the exterminator at the door, she didn't want him to see the gruesomely laid out kitchen. "Hello sir, I seem to have a bit of a rat infestation like we talked about over the phone." She cried to the man as he approached her. "Okay well where are they now?" he replied. "I believe they have gone back outside somewhere now, but they did a number on my kitchen. I killed as many of them as possible. I warn you before you come in, it is still a mess." she said, trembling.

The man followed her inside and immediately covered his nose and started to gag. "Oh my god that smell," the man said, "yes I know it's quite awful, the rats looked diseased," she remarked. "Did you get bit at all because if so, you might want to get a rabies shot to be safe," he said before walking back outside to get fresh air.

She followed behind him, checking her arms and legs, "I don't believe so, I'm pretty sure I was the one doing all of the destruction, besides them eating my food and chewing through my cabinets and wall." she said. The man chuckled, "Well okay I can work on spraying the perimeter and work on plugging any holes I see in the wall or near doorways to deter them. I'll let you know when I'm done," the man said before grabbing his tools from his truck. "Thank you," Barb replied, she then propped the front door open and went back to mopping up the mess of a kitchen.

On the far side of town Noah was getting ready for war, he packed a fresh inhaler along with hair spray and a lighter as his main weapon. He also brought a bottle of water and a small bag of cheese balls to snack on. Now all he had to do was sneak out at the perfect time through his window when his parents were eating dinner.

Emma didn't know what to bring or what to grab. She ended up packing a bag full of medical supplies that ranged from band-aids, gauze and even hydrogen peroxide to clean wounds. She felt like no one else was going to be bringing those items, so she decided to bring them herself.

Josie and David ended up grabbing loads of food from the pantry and multiple flashlights. One bag was going to be full of food and the other was going to be full of tools. In the tool bag they packed a whistle, two flashlights, a matchbox and a couple kitchen knives to protect them.

Charleston and Evan both had the same idea. They filled their bags with multiple water jugs in the event they got stuck and needed to stay alive. Charleston ended up bringing a hand-made spear he had made months ago. Evan on the other hand had a dagger that was passed down to him and kept on the wall. Neither of them could put their weapon in their bag so they would have to carry them without getting caught.

After Harold wrote his letter and laid down for a minute to gather his thoughts, he grabbed his guitar in the closet, "hey you old thing," dusting it off. He then went into the kitchen, grabbed a flashlight and a few boxes of crackers. He also grabbed a hammer from his mom's toolbox and put it in his bag. He zipped his bag, throwing it over his shoulder, grabbed his guitar then put his boots back on and left through the back door.

Emma left fifteen minutes early and walked over to the graveyard. She sat down next to her father's headstone, "Hi daddy, I am going on a mission with friends tonight. I'm asking for your strength and protection because it might be dangerous. I love you very much." she prayed. She kissed her hand then touched her dad's headstone, got up and began to walk to the tree line.

All the other kids began heading to the meet up point. They all arrived and gathered around Harold again hoping he would make a speech to help them calm their nerves. "This is it guys, what we have been waiting for…preparing for. I know we might be walking into something bad, but if we stick together, we can defeat anything. I believe in you all, now who's with me?! Let's do this," Harold said, passionately. The kids all chanted and raised their weapons before marching into the woods.

Ms. Jackson was finishing up cleaning in her kitchen, the exterminator had left and she was taking a breather. She heard an echo from the kids conversing, looked out of her back window and saw the kids walking into the woods again. "What are they doing? Do I follow again? I can't bear to see them get hurt…they even have weapons?! Screw this…I'm going." She huffed. Ms. Jackson grabbed her coat and headed outside.

The kids made their way into the gully, and all the sudden rain began to fall heavily. "Should we turn back?" Noah wailed. "No, we cannot show weakness," Harold replied. They finally arrived at the stream and Harold helped everyone jump one by one. Once they all got into the water Ms. Jackson had made her way into the woods. She wanted to follow them, but the rain was making it hard to keep her footing. The rain became heavier and lightning took over the sky.

Harold was leading the pack and about to walk into the tunnel, guitar in hand knowing he had to stay strong. The other kids made a train behind him and followed him inside. Ms. Jackson eventually got to the stream and could see one of the kids' schoolbags going deeper into the tunnel. She hopped down into the stream, followed them slowly and stopped halfway inside the tunnel. Ms. Jackson saw the kids stop at what looked to be an entangled nesting of roots, she wondered what this place could be.

"Go for it Harold, the rain is pounding us," Charleston said. Harold put his guitar strap over his shoulder and took a deep breath, "I hope this works." He grabbed his guitar and began to strum in the key of G. The ground started to tremble, and the vines started to move. Everyone was standing around bracing themselves for the entrance to open.

He played louder, harder, until the ground shook violently. The vines opened from side to side and Harold looked at the others nodding for them to get ready to go in. The kids lined up as soon as the vines and roots pulled away and they took a step inside. Harold continued strumming while walking forward until he was also inside, then he suddenly stopped playing. The vines tangled and spun back together and made a loud snapping noise as the ground stopped shaking, closing the door behind them.

"That's it, we're in" Emma said. Ms. Jackson couldn't believe her eyes, she felt bewildered. Astonished by the power of the kids and the whimsical roots that they moved. She made her way through the remainder of the tunnel and stood up next to the doorway. The kids couldn't help but feel in awe of their surroundings.

On all sides the Castle was encased with pine trees that bent and waved in bizarre ways. In the middle was a huge pine tree, unlike any they had seen before. To the left of the tree there was a small graveyard that looked decayed and abandoned. To the right there was a crypt that appeared to go underground. "Okay, let's look around but be careful," Harold said. The kids acknowledged him and started roaming around.

"Look, Emma!" Josie shouted while pointing at the huge pine tree. Emma followed her over and they saw a small sword with a wooden handle sticking out of the tree. Josie grabbed the handle with both hands and yanked it free. She closely inspected the blade, and it read *S. Noelle* on the lower half. "Huh I wonder who that could be?"

Josie said. "Well, it must have been a mighty woman of some sort." Emma uttered.

Noah, Evan and Charleston were all on the right side looking at the crypt and trying to figure out how to open it. The crypt had moss hanging on all sides and behind a thin layer of dirt was a note.

Do not open for any reason, must stay underground.

"Huh, I wonder why." Evan asked. No matter what angle they tried looking at it, the crypt appeared to be sealed from the inside out. They gave up and walked back over to Emma and Josie.

David and Harold were over on the left side checking out the graveyard. All the tombstones had no names. They saw only one that had a name on it, they wiped away the grime covering it so they could get a better look.

Rest In Peace 1902-1937

Sarah Noelle

"She must be the only one buried here and the other graves must be empty," David noted. "Hey guys come look at this sword," Noah shouted to

Harold and David. They both made their way over to the tree, "Look it says S. Noelle, I wonder who she is?" Josie said. "The tombstone over there says Sarah Noelle, so it must've been her sword," Harold commented. They all then walked over to the tombstone and speculated why she was the only one buried here.

Noah happened to stay at the tree because he saw what looked like a small window in the bark that he could open. He started to peel back the edge and to his surprise a small cubby was inside. "Guys! Guys…You need to see this; there is something weird in this tree." Noah shouted frantically. They ran back over, Harold got down on his knee to be eye level with the hollowed tree. What he saw inside shocked him.

Harold was looking at a small cube that looked like a gemstone. It was wrapped in roots that looked like ribbon. It was glowing and sitting on a small pedestal of heartwood. Behind it carved into the tree was a short message.

Here Lies the Cube of Faith

those who dare take hold of the cube,

Dare to wield their power

Bestow light and breathe in darkness.

Harold didn't fully understand what this
message meant but that wasn't stopping him. He
reached over the cube, grabbed it and suddenly
everything changed.

8

THE RECKONING

A loud crackle of thunder, a sound of bellowing roars from beneath the ground, and a cry from the murder of crows in the trees. All the kids looked frightened and snared. They couldn't help but notice the vast change the moment Harold decided to grab the cube.

Harold pulled his hand away holding the cube and felt a sense of power fill his body. He couldn't describe it, "Harold what did you do bro?" Noah said. "I don't know, I took the cube…maybe…I shouldn't have. It said something about darkness, but I couldn't resist finding out," he explained. The crows started to swarm them, the roars beneath came closer until they heard a loud thud knock on the door of the crypt. It was at this moment Harold realized he awoke something bad.

Noah took his lighter and hairspray and began torching the crows swarming above them, "Burn!... Burn you little butt munches!", "Quick, the entrance is opening back up guys, we have to go," Emma shouted. The kids all gathered fighting off the crows attacking overhead and made their way back to the entrance. Once they walked out a loud crippling laugh from inside ran chills down their spines. The crypt door had opened, and thousands of decaying rats fled from below.

The kids were panicking in fright, not knowing what this all meant. Ms. Jackson was hiding behind a tree once she heard the roaring, "Kids! What is happening!" she yelled at them. They were startled by her and drew their weapons, "Ms. Jackson? What are you doing here! It's not safe, we need to leave now!" David demanded. Ms. Jackson came out from behind the tree, linking up with the kids, helping fend off the crows.

"Ha-ha, you thought you could get us that easily!" Noah said manically while trying to use the fire from the hairspray, but the rain had other plans. Eventually he couldn't even spark a flame from the lighter. The crows swooped down and pecked at their heads, cawing loudly mocking them.

"Everyone in the tunnel now!" Harold hollered. Ms. Jackson helped all the kids into the tunnel and followed behind while Harold stood at the entrance of the Castle. He felt shameful and felt like this was all his fault, but he didn't know what to do now. Before he was about to walk away, he looked over.

Standing over the thousands of rats scurrying towards them, an army of ghouls that had rotten skin and bones exposed. They looked as though they were dead for many years.

Harold turned around and bolted to the tunnel, gripping his hammer with one hand and the cube of faith in the other. He shouted at the others ahead, "Guys, we have a big problem here, undead! There are undead things coming from the crypt." The kids all paused and waited for Harold on the other side.

Evan grabbed his hand and helped Harold up, "what do you mean?" he murmured. "I saw undead creatures with bones hanging and flesh missing, they are coming this way now." Harold replied. The kids all leaned in and looked back through the tunnel. They saw creatures that had missing skin and half of their faces morphed. "Those are ghouls! I've read about them in books!" Noah called out before eagerly puffing his inhaler. "Kids we must do something; we can't let them get up to the town. People are sleeping right now, they are in danger," Ms. Jackson said. The kids stopped for a second to gather themselves.

They formed a plan to hold the tree line up ahead where the gully meets the field. "Go, go, go!" Harold said, trying to get everyone up the gully as

fast as possible. It was extremely slippery, everyone
kept falling and grabbing branches of trees to get
up. At this time the rats had made their way to the
kids and started gnawing at their ankles, "Get off of
me!" David cried while shaking them off his leg.
Harold started swinging his hammer protecting his
friends from the rats.

All a sudden Harold let out a battle cry, the cube
started to glow brighter, and a sonic boom came
from his mouth. Hundreds of rats and crows keeled
over and died instantly. Everyone stopped for a
second and looked at Harold with batty eyes.

It looked as though the Cube of Faith was
giving him a powerful voice that could eliminate the
undead rats and crows. Harold felt exuberant and
told everyone, "Get out of here, now!" they all
rushed up the hill without wasting a second. Harold
decided to stay in the middle between them and the
ghouls, ready to lay waste to all undead.

He took a look and saw the ghouls coming out
of the tunnel, peering up at him. There was a total
of seven ghouls but one appeared to be bigger than
all the other ones. Harold waited for them to get a
bit closer until he could see their crooked jaws
hanging from their faces. The ghouls started to
sprint in his direction until he powered up and let

out another battle cry, "Aaaaah!" he shouted. The first couple of ghouls busted at their joints and bones flew in all directions. Harold smirked, turned around and sprinted back up to the field.

Once Harold made his way back to everyone, they all hugged him. "It's the cube guys, it has magical powers," Harold muttered. They all looked at one another, "okay what's the game plan now?" Emma asked. "I don't know how many more creatures are going to attack, I think it's best we all hide out in the school. Go and gather everyone and bring them to the school for safety. I will hold the line here." Harold demanded.

Ms. Jackson wanted to protect everyone, but considering he had some sort of cube in his hand that gave him super abilities, she agreed to the plan. "Come on kids, let's go get your parents and wake everyone up. I know it's the middle of the night, but this is urgent so, let's go!" she said. The kids started to follow her saying "Goodluck," to Harold before walking away.

Noah stayed behind a second and put his hands on Harold's shoulders, "I believe in you bro, remember we are here for you. Meet us inside when you are done." Noah said before following the others. After everyone had walked away, Harold turned back to the woods and braced himself for war.

Waves of crows kept dashing his direction, trying to leave the wood line and go into town. He would let out a fierce shout every time a group tried to make their way through. Rats began to climb trees and jump onto Harold as he would swipe them with his hammer, decimating them. "Is this all you got? Bring it on! I can do this all night," he vociferated.

Three more ghouls came over the edge with one larger ghoul behind them. The large one snarled, "Get him!" They started to charge Harold with claws swinging and fangs dripping. Harold tightened his grip on his hammer and on the Cube before swinging at the first ghoul. Harold knocked the ghoul out cold; he then performed a spin attack on the second one. Harold let out a loud roar that made the third ghoul fall to the ground crying in pain. He stood back up and now it was one vs one.

"I see you have adapted the power quite well boy," The remaining ghoul said. "Who are you and what do you want?" Harold replied. "We want the cube! Give it here and we will let you live," the ghoul Snickered. Harold looked down at the cube in his hand and thought to himself, "If this gave me powers, it must give anyone who holds it powers. I can't let them have it,", "how about no," Harold said. "Well, I guess you chose death young one," the ghoul snapped, raising his wooden staff.

The ghoul summoned what looked like a spirit of a raging bull, it charged at Harold running through him, knocking him to the ground. Harold got back up, powered his voice and let out a sonic boom that pierced the ears of the ghoul until the ghoul was on its knees. Harold walked closer, keeping his voice throttled, he took his hammer and drove it into the skull of the ghoul. "We will return," The ghoul hissed before collapsing. Harold dropped his hammer and fell.

Harold felt very low on energy and knew that the cube was likely to blame. "What did it mean, we will return?" he thought. For the time being there was a moment of peace. The rain had slowed down and no more crows nor rats were about. Harold stood up, grabbed his hammer and started walking to the school.

While he was fighting, all the kids and Ms. Jackson gathered everyone up, bringing them to the school. Every house they had knocked on freaked out, unknowing as to why they had to leave. Most people didn't want to go but it seemed urgent, so they followed.

Once they all arrived at the school people began asking questions, "why are we here?", "Is there a natural disaster or something?" They commented. "No, everyone it's much worse, there are undead creatures coming back to life from the woods and trying to attack us." Noah shouted. People started to chuckle, including Emma's stepdad, "Emma do you believe this? Come on, let's go back home," he demanded as he tugged on her arm. She stood her ground, "No, this is actually real, believe it or not, we all are in danger." Emma replied. Everyone just kept laughing, visibly annoyed by the disturbance, they decided to leave back to their homes. Most of the kids' parents grabbed them and brought them back home.

"I knew they wouldn't believe us," Evan whispered to Ms. Jackson. "Yes, well, it doesn't sound very believable," She stated. "What do we do now?" Josie asked, "it's only you, Evan and I,", "Well we wait here for Harold just like he said to do." Ms. Jackson replied. The double doors at the side of the school abruptly opened and Harold was on the other side.

They rushed over to him, noticing he was fatigued and looked like hell. "Are you okay?" Ms. Jackson said, worried. "Yes, I'm fine, I fought them off for now. One of them spoke and said they will return, I don't know when or how, but we must always be ready. Where are the others?" Harold asked. "They didn't believe us, they left." Evan said. Harold dropped back down to the ground, "I need to rest really quick." They all sat down next to him and waited for him to recover.

In the field where the battle had just taken place, the ghouls reanimated back to life. A swarm of rats and a murder of crows flew towards the neighborhood ready to wreak havoc. The ambassador ghoul ordered the recruits, "Find me the cube, we must bring it back to our lord," the ghouls screeched in synchronicity.

Most of the people in the neighborhood had just made their way back to bed, except for all the children. They remained awake and wanted to head back to school because they saw the undead with their own eyes. Suddenly crows started slamming into everyone's windows, one by one fragmenting the glass until it shattered. The rats chewed through the bottom corners of doors until they reached the inside of homes. People started to panic as the chaos ensued, it left them now believing what Noah had said.

"I told you guys! You didn't listen." Emma said to her parents. Her stepdad paused and was in disbelief, he ended up realizing they must go back to the school. Everyone made their way outside, stepping over rats that had rotten flesh hanging off their bodies. The crows continued to pester the town as they all made their way back to the school.

Harold seemed to finally be catching his breath and stood back up, "we need to find out when they are coming back. He told me they are after this cube, we cannot let them have it," Harold said. Evan, Josie and Ms. Jackson all stood up with Harold and heard what sounded like someone screaming. "Help, please help," They ran to the front door, opened it and saw the streets flooded with rats and crows. They noticed everyone running towards them, "I have to help them," Harold said before stepping outside.

As they all neared the entrance, Harold told them, "Get inside now! Go…go!" before harnessing the power and letting out a ferocious shout that sent shockwaves through the streets. Rats blew up, crows fell to the tar, but he couldn't help but notice shadows in the distance. Everyone was now inside the school and safe, most of them sobbing with minor wounds scattered all over their bodies.

Josie and Ms. Jackson went back outside to check on Harold and noticed he was starting to become fatigued again. It will only be so long until he collapses and potentially drops the cube. A loud voice belched from over in the woods. "Give me my cube!" Harold was ready to fight the ghouls once more.

The ghouls in the distance charged him until Harold used his power to demolish them. The Ambassador ghoul summoned another bull that charged and knocked Harold, Josie and Ms. Jackson over. Harold was out of energy and dropped the cube of faith, in a split-second Josie picked it up.

Josie took the cube and stood up; she felt a powerful surge of holy energy fill her body. The Ghoul raised his wooden staff and started to initiate a spell. Before the spell went off, Josie took her hand as if she was throwing a ball and launched a bolt of holy fire at the ghoul. The ghoul grabbed its face in agony as she belted him with another bolt. The ambassador ghoul finally fell and perished once more.

Josie dropped the cube and helped Harold to his feet, "That was incredible you two," Ms. Jackson cheered. "I got you," Josie said to Harold, "thank you, good job," he replied, struggling to breathe. It appeared they had killed all the ghouls once again and simmered the fire. Once Harold got to his feet, he hugged Josie then picked the cube back up off the ground. They turned around and went to walk back inside when they felt the ground shake beneath their feet, something was stomping in their direction.

They looked back at the road and saw a tall, slender ghoul three times the size of the others. It was wearing a black robe and had a small scepter with a skull on the end of it. The ghoul also had a ring of fire around its head that took the shape of a crown.

"I believe you have something that belongs to me?" the ghoul said. "Who are you? I'm not giving you the cube…ever!" Harold shrieked. "I am the sorcerer of night, the bringer of death, the one who destroys all in his path…Lord Gohpug." The ghoul replied. Harold and Josie stood tall, unafraid of his aura, ready to fight.

"We are not giving you the cube, you will have to take it from our dead bodies!" Harold shouted. "Very well then child," Gohpug replied. Lord Gohpug raised his scepter and cast a fireball that hit

Harold directly in his arm causing him to drop the cube of faith. Harold screamed in pain as his arm was melting from the flames, Josie picked up the cube. She began firing bolts of holy fire at Gohpug, he used his scepter to block the spells and unleash fire from beneath their feet. The ground began to char underneath them. Josie, Harold and Ms. Jackson ran back inside.

Once they got back inside of the school, Harold's arm was beginning to cave in. Josie dropped the cube of faith and held him close, "you're going to be okay." she cried, everyone stood back and watched in shock. Curious of what her powers might be, Ms. Jackson grabbed the cube. She felt empowered with restoration. She kneeled and put her hand on Harold's molten arm; it started to heal. Josie couldn't believe her eyes, and neither could the others. Harold's arm fully healed and he hugged Ms. Jackson tightly, "thank you, that was incredible." he said, before getting back up.

Outside Lord Gohpug was resurrecting his ghouls, "rise ambassador and bring your army with you," he spoke. The ghouls rose and reanimated back to life. They started marching towards the school when they noticed the sun rising. Lord Gohpug looked up at the sky and saw that the night was near an end, "Everyone get back to the castle, quickly!" he demanded. All the ghouls including Gohpug ran back into the woods and disappeared into the crypt.

Now that Harold's arm was fully restored and nobody else was hurt, it was time to open the doors again and fight Lord Gohpug. All his friends gathered with him, "we are with you Harold," David said. Harold opened the front door of the school, ready for the worst to happen. To their surprise there was nothing in sight, not a dead bird nor rat.

They noticed the sun peaking over the trees. Harold looked up at the sky then back down to the road. "The sorcerer of night…they must only be able to come out at nighttime, I guess," Harold concluded, saying his thoughts out loud. Everyone looked relieved because they needed a break to process everything. They went back inside the school to recuperate.

9

The Day After

Dawn had finally come, the townspeople were sleepy-eyed, dazed and scared. Many of them felt like they had a bad dream. Amidst the madness, Harold totally forgot to make sure his mother was okay, he looked around the hallway and saw his mom in the back, "Momma!" He shouted. She rubbed her eyes then got up, "Harold, baby you're safe!" She ran to him, kissing his forehead. "I missed you momma," Harold said while wrapping his arms around her. Ms. Jackson was happy to see everyone here and that no one went missing.

Harold pulled away from his mom to give an announcement, "Listen up everyone, these things we are fighting right now only come out at nighttime. You can do whatever you want today, but I want everyone to meet me in the field behind the Huffington house in a couple hours. These creatures will come back, and we must be ready to fight them tomorrow night." Everyone was half awake, barely listening but they agreed agreement.

All the kids gathered around Harold and Josie. "That was epic what you did, I've only ever seen stuff like that in comic books," Noah cheered. Josie giggled and felt like a hero. "Okay guys we finally found out what is behind the vined doorway, tonight will be the night where we kill the leader of the undead army. I'll see you all in the field in a couple hours, go home and rest because we are going to devise a plan," Harold said before turning around and walking home with his mother.

Many of the townspeople started to make their way back to their homes with the kids falling behind to talk with Ms. Jackson. "That was amazing how you healed Harold like that," Emma said, "I still don't believe it happened." Ms. Jackson replied. Josie looked over at Ms. Jackson, "Do you think we can take Lord Gohpug? We only saw him for like a minute and he almost got us.", "Yes Josie I believe we can do anything as long as we stick together." Ms. Jackson said before wrapping her arms around Josie tightly. They all walked outside and felt empowered. Even though they discovered some grueling secrets of their little town Elvingdale, they knew they could accomplish the unthinkable with the cube.

Families arrived back home as the sun was almost fully in the sky, the kids shortly after. "Love you momma, I'm glad I get to see you for another day." Harold said, relieved. She smiled back at him before she went back to bed. Harold got to his room, exhausted from the long night. He looked at the note on his table he made and thought he might as well keep it there since tonight would prove to be a tougher fight.

He laid down feeling comfortable on his mattress. He had so much built-up tension in his body and became rather stiff. He grabbed the cube with both of his hands, twirling it over his head, thinking to himself how incredible it truly was.

The saying he found behind the cube never slipped his mind. He pondered, starting to doubt they would be able to even win against Lord Gohpug. After all he was a sorcerer and that was his home, so he very well knew the powers the cube could give off. Harold was lying restlessly, unable to sleep for a wink, he got back up and decided to head to the Castle of Pine alone.

It was morning now so there was no chance of running into the ghouls. He wanted to head back to see if he could uncover anything else, any other secrets that would be helpful. He found his way back into the woods until he reached the stream, then made his way through the tunnel to the Castle.

Once he arrived at the entrance, he noticed small flowers blooming all around the vines and ground inside the Castle. He was stunned by their beauty, it felt like they were singing vibrant, decadent songs to him.

He was busy looking at the ground, feeling like he was dreaming. "We haven't been here during the day? It feels much different." He whispered. Finally snapping out of the trance, Harold looked up at the enormous pine tree and his jaw dropped. It was sparkling like a diamond; the tree looked like a piece of jewelry on a queen's neck. He walked up to it and ran his fingers through the bark. Harold never thought they would see the inside of the Castle, let alone find a cube that has magical powers.

He walked slowly around the tree, looking for etchings or distinguishable features, but nothing caught his eye, all he saw was the sword Josie put back in the tree. His back was to the crypt when he randomly heard a voice, "hello," it said. He stopped, afraid to turn his head around. "Hello, young man," it said again, at this time he realized it was a woman's voice. He finally built the courage to turn around.

There was a woman standing by the doorway of the crypt, on top of the fallen door. She was transparent and had a light shimmer around her. "H…h…hello ma'am," Harold said nervously. She walked closer to him, "are you the one who took the cube?" she asked. Not knowing if he should answer the question honestly, he replied, "Maybe.", "Oh…no" she cried. Harold knew that he may have made a mistake, considering the ghouls nearly destroyed the town.

"I know I probably should have left it, but I didn't think about the consequences when I grabbed it. I saw how beautiful it was, and it pulled me in," he said to her. "Yes, that was the same problem I had," She replied. Harold raised his eyebrow and felt more comfortable knowing that she also fell victim to the cube. "You did? Who are you?" he asked. "I am Sarah Noelle, the first and only person to have grabbed the cube before you. I found this castle when I went for long walks in the woods alone and just like you, felt the need to explore it." she replied.

Harold stood there flabbergasted. Noticing her shimmer and how she was practically see-through, he asked "are you…a…ghost?"," why yes, I am, I am trapped here forever. All I can do is walk around this Castle, if I try to go outside of it there is an invisible wall that prevents me from leaving." she replied. This made Harold think about the crows that would run into imaginary walls in the sky and fall to the ground. He had so many questions for her but didn't want to be rude.

"I'm guessing by now you have discovered the powers the cube can give you?" she inquired. "Yes…yes we have, so far three of us have incredible abilities that are all different when we possess the cube," he replied. Sarah paced back and forth, "Okay well you must defeat Lord Gohpug, if you cannot defeat him there is only one other way to have the nightmare end." she stated.

Harold stuttered and asked "di…did you defeat him?", "No I did not, sadly I had to take another route that left me here forever. The night I took the cube; I ended up staying in here because the sounds ran throughout my body. They held me captive and made me feel paralyzed. It was only just before the crypt opened that I realized what was happening," she paused.

"Monsters started to flood from beneath the crypt, and I initially was running around in circles to get away from them, until I tapped into the cubes power. I had the ability to destroy things with my mind just by looking at them and blinking, so for the first couple of ghouls, rats, and crows, that's what I did. It eventually became so overwhelming

115

that I didn't know what to do and wanted the nightmare to end already. I did the only thing I thought would work and that was to return the cube of faith to its original spot," She paused again, taking a deep breath.

"Once I did that, a beam of light destroyed all the undead creatures and reset the doorway of the crypt. I thought I was finally safe, but once I looked down, I noticed that I no longer had a body. I tried to touch my face, but my hand just went through, like I wasn't even there but I was," she said as she started to cry.

"It took me a couple minutes of figuring it out. I then concluded that if you want to return the cube, you must sacrifice your own life. I walked over to where the little graveyard was that had no names on the headstones and magically my name was written on one of them. You must defeat Lord Gohpug if you want to stay alive," Sarah said. Harold dropped to his knees, crying from her heartbreaking story.

Sarah could tell that it was a lot of information for him to take in, he was only a kid, and she was an adult when this happened. She kneeled and said, "I know you guys can defeat Lord Gohpug. Find out everyone's special powers when they have the cube and utilize them to destroy him once and for all."

Harold wiped away his tears and was extremely thankful for the information Sarah had given him. "Thank you so much, I'm so sorry this happened to you. I will do the best I can to destroy him and put an end to this madness," he said as he stood back up.

After their conversation he waved goodbye to Sarah Noelle and walked back through the stream. Harold felt like a new man and was ready to foolproof a strategy to destroy Lord Gohpug. Once he got back home, he put the cube of faith on his table next to his note for momma tree, he laid down and tried to rest for the remaining hour before they would all meet in the field.

An hour had passed and everyone woke up. The town felt still and the air was dense, worry took over the minds of most people. They still had glass from the shattered windows throughout their homes, chewed fragments of wood missing from their doors. This wouldn't be easy to get everyone to work together, but if anyone could do it, it would be the kids.

Everyone got to the field and sat down except for the kids. The kids stood at the front of the townspeople with Ms. Jackson, waiting for Harold and his mother to arrive. "Alright momma let's do this," Harold said before grabbing his mother's hand. "Let's go baby, I believe in you." she replied. They made their way over to everyone; Momma tree sat down with the others and Harold walked up to the front.

"I know most of you don't know what's happening right now, so let me fill you in. Our friend group found a magical fortress in the woods that contained this cube," he held the cube up in the air for all to see. "This cube contains powers that differ from person to person, we do not know how many people can have these powers or what they will be, but they are insane. Once I took the cube from the fortress, called the Castle of Pine, I woke up those creatures you all saw last night. They will come back every night until we kill their leader, Lord Gohpug," Harold announced.

One of the townspeople shouted, "So it's your fault we're in danger?", "any one of us could have grabbed this cube, it just happened to be Harold," Emma riposted. The townspeople started to talk amongst themselves, "I was the one who found the cube first, so if you want to blame somebody, blame me!" Noah shouted. "There is no use arguing, what's done is done. We must come together now to defeat the evil creatures coming for us. If we don't, they will terrorize our town every night until there is nothing left," Ms. Jackson said. Everyone went quiet and recognized that they needed to work together.

Harold put the cube back down by his side. "First things first, we are going to find out what abilities each person has and go from there. Form a line and we will begin," he said. Everyone got into a line and the kids were first to try.

David stepped up and grabbed the cube, but nothing happened, no abilities or anything. Harold thought it was odd but continued to the next person. Noah grabbed the cube and thought for sure he was going to have something happen, but again nothing happened. He gave the cube back to Harold and huffed.

Evan stepped up and grabbed the cube; he felt immense power and his hand suddenly became a long sword made of light. He was shocked and returned the cube to Harold. "Okay it looks like some people will have abilities and others will not," Harold shouted.

They continued down the line, Emma was next. She grabbed the cube and again, nothing happened. Next up was Charleston, once he grabbed the cube he felt a surge of power. He slightly lifted his foot off the ground, and a small earthquake began to rumble beneath them. Harold quickly took the cube back, "yep, that's good enough," he said, making everyone laugh. They already knew that Ms. Jackson and Josie had abilities, so the rest of the line consisted of the townspeople and their parents.

One by one they came up. Every single time one of them tried, nothing would happen. An hour went by and they had one person left in line, Momma tree. After all the failed attempts, she didn't look confident at all.

She grabbed the cube from her son and instantly started levitating. She leaned over and began to fly around, zipping through the field at incredible speeds. Everyone's jaw dropped to the ground in awe; she returned to her son and gave Harold the cube. "Momma, that was so cool!" Harold chortled, "I told you I always had superpowers baby," she said while laughing. They concluded testing and now it was time to come up with a plan.

Midday had passed and Harold looked up at the sky to locate the sun. He looked back down at the crowd of people, "Okay everyone! We now know who has special powers when holding the cube and who does not. I think it would be best if everyone without abilities stays back inside their homes, while the rest of us fight the creatures out here."

Harold announced. "Well, what about my son, I'm not going to leave him in danger," said Mr. Mire, "Dad, I'll be okay, we need to work together to accomplish this," Charleston replied. "We will all protect each other, no one will be left out, I promise," said Ms. Jackson. Harold's mom backed this notion and put her arms around all the kids.

Now that the townspeople were all on the same page, most of them felt relieved that they didn't have to fight. They wanted to hide and stay as far away from trouble as possible. Since they all agreed on who would take the lion's share, the mass of townsfolk all walked back to their homes. All the kids, including Ms. Jackson and Momma Tree stayed, huddling up to create a bulletproof strategy.

"I want to help, I know I don't have any super ability but please let me help," Noah begged, "Same" said Emma, "me too!" said David. All the others looked at them and saw how much they wanted to be part of the team. It was impossible to deny them, after all they started the journey together, might as well end it together too. "Of course, you guys can help us, we will need every bit of help we can get." Harold said. He then sat down and gestured for the others to sit with him.

121

Harold wanted to share with them the time he spent in the Castle of Pine alone earlier today, but he didn't want to worry everyone. Instead, he hardened up and pushed the pain down inside, so that they could come up with a strategy to try and end Lord Gohpug.

"Okay so what's the plan?" Charleston said, "Moments before nightfall, we will meet here and hold the front line of our town, Preventing Lord Gohpug from entering the town to destroy it. Since we know what all our abilities are now, I think it's best if we stagger into some sort of barrier," Harold said. He was nervous, thinking to himself if this plan would even work.

Noah took a puff of his inhaler, "so where do you want me?" he said, "well…you don't have any powers so I think you should stay back, if any of us get hurt you can try to run and pull us out of harm's way," Harold replied. Noah looked at him and concurred, "That goes for you to Emma and David. If anyone gets hurt, it's important we keep them safe while someone else takes the cube and holds the line," Harold declared. "We only have one cube, so only one person can use their abilities at a time." Josie mentioned, reminding them to balance back and forth.

Momma Tree couldn't help but look at her son and admire his strength. He never talked so much, around the house Harold was always quiet and respectful. She was so proud to see him take charge and become a strong leader; nothing could make her happier. "I love you so much baby," she said, interrupting the conversation randomly. Harold looked at her and he smiled, knowing how much he loved her too.

"I will be first to hold the line, second will be Charleston since he can disrupt the ground. Third will be Evan then fourth, Josie, Momma and Ms. Jackson. If I need help, I will toss the cube back to one of you. Remember we all do different things, call the name of who you are passing the cube to then throw it," Harold said. Emma took a deep breath and had a bad feeling in her gut, but she kept it to herself.

After the conversation was done and they had decided on the structure of the barrier they planned to create, they got up. "Let's all go home and try our best to relax, it's going to be a long night, we need our rest," Ms. Jackson said. Everyone felt overwhelmed, knowing that if they failed, the town would be desecrated for good. They all went their separate ways and walked back home.

10

Final Battle

The day was nearing night; the townspeople were all on edge waiting in their houses. No one was sure if they would make it through the night. A looming sense of dread was plaguing the town. All the kids grabbed the same weapons they had from the night prior and prepared themselves for war.

Charleston made sure to sharpen his spearhead, meanwhile Noah was at home pacing back and forth. Evan was hyping himself up in the mirror, ready for whatever came his way. Harold was just getting out of bed after taking a nap, he was oddly relaxed for the situation. David and Josie had been spending quality time with their parents, laughing, playing board games, trying to distract themselves and keeping spirits high.

It was safe to say everyone had their way of dealing with the pressure. Emma was the only one who never actually went back home, instead she laid next to her dad's tombstone in the graveyard behind the mall. She stayed there for hours looking up at the sky and counting the clouds. Tears rolled down her face as she noticed nighttime was near. Emma wiped her face and sniffled, she got off the ground and waved goodbye to her dad.

Harold walked over to his desk and looked at the note, taking a deep breath, he grabbed the cube of faith. It was almost time for them to hold the line and protect the city. He walked into the kitchen and saw Momma Tree; she was radiating with love. Harold smiled when he saw her energy, it made him stronger seeing her so positive. "Are you ready Momma?" Harold asked, "Yes sweetie, let's do this." She replied. They walked out of the back door, Harold looked back at his home, knowing it might be the last time he had got to see it.

Ms. Jackson was just about ready. She grabbed her broom and broke it over her knee; it was now a weapon with a jagged tip. She went into her bedroom and found Snuggles, "hi baby, momma loves you," she said, stuffing her face into the side of his fur. Ms. Jackson gave him plenty of tickles, listening to him purr, it was the only thing keeping her calm before the battle. "I love you snuggles, no matter what, you are the best cat anyone could have," she said to him before walking out of her house.

The sun was beginning to set, and everyone was getting ready for war. One by one the kids started to arrive at the meeting point in the field. They all nodded at each other; it was a sign of showing readiness. Emma was the last one to arrive, waving at everyone. The parents of Emma, David and Josie all watched from inside their homes cowering for safety. Finally, the sun began to set, and dusk was around the corner.

Minutes before the sun was about to fade away, Evan walked up to Josie. He grabbed her hand, "In case we don't make it, I need you to know how I feel about you," He leaned in and kissed her on the lips. The world disappeared for a second and everything felt peaceful, Josie was in heaven, she ended up wrapping her arms around him.

Evan pulled away and smiled shyly; Josie looked back at him with the brightest smile. "Was it you all along?" Josie said, "Yes, I left the note in your locker, everything started happening, so I never got around to tell you," Evan said. She pulled him in closer and nestled her head on his shoulders, everyone else watched in joy.

The sun had finally set; it was nearing the time for the unknown. "No matter what happens here guys, no matter if we lose or if we win, I want you all to know how much I care about you and love you," Harold yelled. Everyone walked over to him and gave him a group hug, "We love you man," Noah said while sobbing, "we are all best friends," Charleston added. While they were overwhelmed with emotion, finally feeling the pressure of the situation, a loud cackle was heard in the distance. Everyone got into positions, preparing their minds for the forces to come.

The sky had turned black; the woods had come alive and there was a moment of silence. Shortly after, a devastatingly loud shriek pierced the ears of everyone, breaking the remaining windows of people's homes. It sounded like it could be Lord Gohpug, but they were unsure. Slowly the sounds of stomping and the smell of rotten flesh neared closer. Harold finally saw the undead creatures in the distance; he looked at the cube and looked back up.

The first wave of rats ran into the field; Harold beckoned his voice and projected a wave of sound that even made the trees feel threatened. A horde of crows started to bum-rush them, swooping down and pecking at their heads. Harold looked up at them and shouted; they fell from the sky just like before. He turned back around, facing the wood line, waiting for the big bad ghouls.

Five ghouls came rushing from the forest, Harold shouted but nothing happened, his powers weakened. They continued sprinting in his direction, "Charleston, catch!" Harold threw the cube and stepped back. Charleston tossed his spear over to Harold then summoned the power from the cube, slamming his foot into the ground causing a powerful surge of energy to break the earth below the ghouls. Several ghouls fell into the cracks of earth, but one remained sprinting at them. Harold came up behind the right side of Charleston and speared the ghoul, pushing him into the crevice. Charleston tossed the cube back to Harold and the fissure below closed, becoming solid again.

"Charge!" the distant voice of Lord Gohpug said in the depths of the woods. Another wave of ghouls came flooding from the trees, again Harold attempted to shout but nothing happened. He was too weak to use his abilities. "Evan, Catch!" Harold threw the cube; Evan caught it and moved up. Josie was so nervous and didn't want him to get hurt but she believed in him.

Evan held the cube tightly in one hand and his other hand became a two-foot-long blade of light. He began to weave through the ghouls, slashing them in half. Suddenly an ambassador ghoul was behind the others, Evan didn't see him. The ambassador struck Evan with his staff, causing Evan to fall to the ground.

Everyone gasped and thought the worst, "Harold, catch!" Evan tossed the cube and it tumbled on the ground in front of Harold. He picked up the cube. Lo and behold he roared at the ambassador and the ghoul froze before falling to the ground in pain.

Harold ran over and helped Evan to his feet, Evan didn't seem to be in the best of shape, but it didn't look serious either. Harold brought Evan all the way back to Ms. Jackson, then tossed her the cube. She put her hands on Evans' leg, and it healed instantly, she then did the same with his chest. His pain vanished and he returned to the battle.

While Ms. Jackson was healing Evan, Charleston was holding the front line. He had his spear in hand, gouging at the remaining ghouls. "Is that it? You guys are weak!" Charleston shouted, ending the final ghoul with his spear. He looked down and counted eleven ghouls, "How many more are there?" Charleston asked. Harold took the cube back from Ms. Jackson and walked over to Charleston, they had a brief minute to rest.

"Dude, there are eleven ghouls here already…how many more can there be?" Charleston said, "I'm not sure, all I know is that Lord Gohpug can revive them somehow," Harold replied. They continued to catch their breath and gather their thoughts.

A ring of fire began to make its way through the trees, Harold knew it was Lord Gohpug. "Children, children, why do you never learn?" Gohpug said as he made his way into the field, stomping heavily. Everyone was stunned at how tall he was, he had an aura to him that screamed darkness.

"I will ask one more time, give me the cube" Lord Gohpug said while reaching his hand out. Harold looked at his friends then looked back at Gohpug, "We will Never, give you the cube," Harold shouted. Lord Gohpug cracked his undead neck, "fools." He growled, raising his scepter.

Lord Gohpug waved his scepter and a ball of mucus like venom hit Harold's chest. He fell backwards to the ground; the cube had fallen out of his hand. Charleston grabbed the cube and stomped his foot on the ground. Another fissure appeared and Lord Gohpug began to fall into the earth. Emma and Noah ran along the line and dragged Harold back to Ms. Jackson.

Before falling to his death, Lord Gohpug grabbed the side of the fissure and lifted himself back up. "Evan catch," Charleston said, lobbing the cube of faith to Evan then sprinting towards Lord Gohpug with his spear. Charleston drove his spear in the direction of Lord Gohpug, but he dodged it and raised his scepter, casting a fireball directly at Charleston, knocking him to the ground. Lord Gohpug let out a bestial howl and began walking towards Evan.

Evan morphed his hand back into a sword, charging at Lord Gohpug. Evan dove and sliced him causing him to shout from the pain. Evan raised his sword and swung, Lord Gohpug blocked it with his scepter then grabbed Evan's neck, raising him in the air. "You think you can kill me that easily boy?" Lord Gohpug said, spitting bile in his face. Evan squirmed, as he slowly was losing consciousness, his sword morphed back into his hand.

"Josie…catch," Evan threw the cube as hard as he could towards Josie. She caught the cube and hurled bolts of light at Lord Gohpug, stunning him, causing him to drop Evan. Lord Gohpug began to cast fireballs at Josie, but she would block everyone with her bolts of light.

They went back and forth until Evan got back up to his feet, jumping on Lord Gohpug's back, strangling him. Josie sent three bolts through Lord

Gohpug's chest, he stumbled backwards, before ripping Evan off his back. Lord Gohpug summoned scorching fire under Josie's feet, causing her to roll away and stop attacking. "I've had enough of you all, the cube is mine!" Lord Gohpug screamed, enraged. He cast charming spells that hit Emma, Noah and David, making them fall into a deep sleep.

Harold was still on the ground, his whole body was becoming numb, and it was becoming difficult to breathe. Black lines started to form all over his body that looked to be poisoning him from the inside out, there was nothing he could do but lie there. Charleston's chest was caving in from the fireball; he was unable to move and felt like he might die soon. Evan was dazed, struggling to get his bearings after being thrown to the ground. It did not look good for them.

Josie dashed out of the fire and started to build up another bolt of light. Before she could cast it, Lord Gohpug hit her with a ball of venom, causing her to fall to the ground and drop the cube. Momma tree looked over and saw the cube; she dashed over and picked it up. Momma Tree knew that all she had to do was keep the cube far away from Lord Gohpug, so she flew high into the sky. Ms. Jackson was the only person who was left on the ground that wasn't hurt. She waited for Lord Gohpug to get distracted before making a move.

Lord Gohpug saw Momma tree flying high with the cube and he snarled. He reanimated a flock of crows, "Get her!" He told them. The crows began to follow Momma tree and unfortunately for her they were slightly faster. She started to fly towards the school which made Lord Gohpug walk that direction, he paid no mind to Ms. Jackson. Once he walked far enough away, she got up and gathered all the fallen kids into a close proximity. Momma Tree noticed what Ms. Jackson was doing and waited for the perfect moment before swooping down and bringing the cube back to her.

Once Momma Tree landed, Ms. Jackson took the cube and began bringing the kids back to life, fully restoring them. Lord Gohpug saw what they were doing and became agitated. He walked back towards them and ordered the crows to attack. Momma Tree stood up, punching the crows in the beak, protecting the kids and Ms. Jackson. One by one the kids recovered and stood up. They joined Momma Tree, punching until every crow was knocked out.

Lord Gohpug looked at them with frustration in his eyes. Josie grabbed the cube from Ms. Jackson, "hey doofus, you are not going to kill us that easily." She said, mocking Lord Gohpug. Everyone else stood up around her grabbing their weapons. "Very well then," Lord Gohpug said, he then raised his scepter.

Before he could even cast his spell, Josie started flinging bolts at him with great haste. It weakened him enough that he stopped casting, "Harold, go," Josie said and passed the cube to Harold. He stepped closer to Gohpug and let out a fierce war cry that made him fall to his knees and drop his scepter. "Your turn Charleston," Harold threw the cube over to Charleston, he stomped his foot making the ground tremble. A large chasm formed around Lord Gohpug, he was trapped on a small rock in the middle, weakened and unable to fight back.

Charleston continued to hold onto the cube so that the chasm stayed open. He passed his spear to Evan, "End him." Charleston shouted. Evan hurled the spear with the precision of a marksman. The spear went through the chest of Lord Gohpug, he was screaming, "no, this cannot be," as he began to fall back into the chasm. Everyone hugged each other, watching him fall deeper into the chasm.

As they hugged, the sound of crows squawking below caught their attention. Lord Gohpug was falling to his demise when he caught his scepter mid-air and summoned crows at his feet. The crows took on his weight and flew him back to the surface. Lord Gohpug appeared to be completely fine, even with a spear sticking out of his body. The kids were confused on how he wasn't dead, "how is this possible?" Harold said before grabbing the cube back from Charleston.

Lord Gohpug broke the spear and pulled both pieces out of his body. "Enough of the games!" he yelled. He waved his scepter and a charming spell flew to everyone. They all fell to the ground slowly, unable to move, as if they were transformed to stone. The cube fell out of Harold's hand and rolled onto the grass. Lord Gohpug walked over and grabbed the stone off the ground. He put his putrid foot on Harold's stomach, "enjoy watching your town burn." he snarled before walking away.

Lord Gohpug rose his scepter once again, raising all of his ghouls, crows, and rats from the dead. He held the cube in his hand, commanding them all to attack the townspeople. Lord Gohpug raised the cube to the sky, a bright beam of fire shot out from the cube into the clouds. A large, dark cloud formed in the sky and fire rained down on the town. Lord Gohpug began to laugh, nothing could stop him now.

On the ground Ms. Jackson, Momma tree and all of the children were stuck watching the sky. When abruptly, David, Noah and Emma were able to break free from the charming spell. Since all three of them were just under a different charming spell it prevented this one from taking full effect. Lord Gohpug was still distracted with power; the cube was held to the sky as chains of fire fell from above.

"David, we have to do something now," Noah whispered, before he slowly crept up to Lord Gohpug. David grabbed Evans' dagger and snuck up behind Lord Gohpug. Noah walked in front of him, "hey butt munch, eat this," he said before unleashing hair spray into is eyes.

David stuck the dagger deep into his back at the same time Noah used the hair spray. Lord Gohpug grabbed his eyes, dropping the cube. The clouds disappeared and Noah picked the cube up off the ground. Lord Gohpug fell down, groaning, unable to take the dagger out of his back.

David and Noah ran back to everyone else. Noah opened Ms. Jackson's hand and put the cube of faith in her palm. The power of the cube restored her and brought her back to normal. Ms. Jackson got up and healed everyone on the ground, until everyone was renewed.

Harold got off the ground slowly, coughing. He saw that Lord Gohpug was injured again, but he also saw the ghouls, crows and rats were beginning to ravage the town. "Is everyone okay?" Ms. Jackson asked, "yes, it looks like it," Emma replied. There was no time to waste, the town was going to shambles and they needed to act fast.

Lord Gohpug somehow rose to his feet with the dagger still stuck in his back. He grabbed his scepter, "It's not over yet," he said with a menacing tone. Harold knew that this was never going to end, no matter how many times they weakened him. He bowed his head, remembering what Sarah had told him in the Castle of Pine earlier today.

"Give me the cube," Harold said with a sign of defeat in his voice. Ms. Jackson quickly gave him the cube. Everyone noticed Harold seemed different suddenly, "Remember, I love every one of you. We tried to do this the right way, but he's just too strong," Harold said. No one knew what he was getting at, "What do you mean baby?" Momma Tree asked. "I'm going to make things right. it's the only way." Harold replied before turning around and dashing towards the woods.

Lord Gohpug started to cast fireballs at Harold. Harold jumped and dodged them, "Baby, where are you going?" Momma tree said as she started to cry. Evan couldn't stand still, he started chasing after Harold, avoiding the fire. Harold made his way down to the gully, into the stream. "Harold, wait up, what are you doing?" Evan shouted at him. Harold glanced at him quickly then made his way through the tunnel until he reached the Castle.

Everyone who stayed in the field was unsure of what to do. They noticed Lord Gohpug make his way into the woods, following the boys. Harold finally arrived back at the sparkling Pine tree and got down on his knees looking at the cubes pedestal. Evan was walking through the entrance behind Harold, "Dude what are you doing?" Evan asked. "The cube has to be returned to its spot, it's the only way to end all of this," Harold replied with a dismal tone.

Without warning Harold lifted the cube, "I love you Evan, never forget that" he said before quickly putting the cube back on the pedestal. The tree began to glow brightly, and a shockwave of light emitted from all angles.

Evan covered his face until the shockwave ended, only to see that Harold had disappeared. Evan was holding back his tears and looked everywhere for Harold, "dude, where are you…Harold? Bro, come back," he shouted. Evan walked back out of the castle thinking Harold could be there, but he was alone. The vines began moving and tangled together, sealing the doorway shut.

11

Friends Forever

Evan fell to the ground, crying, knowing that Harold had just sacrificed his life to protect the town. He couldn't get over how quickly everything had happened. All he could think to himself is how he will never see his friend ever again. It broke his heart, but unfortunately, he had to share the news with the others.

Everyone who stayed in the field saw the shockwave emit throughout the town. They noticed the ghouls, crows and rats vanished when the shockwave ended. Noah looked at Josie, "What just happened?" he asked, "I'm…not…sure," she replied. They knew something must have taken place within the Castle of Pine. "Guys, let's go see what they are doing down there," Charleston said. Everyone followed him down into the gully and made their way to the tunnel.

Once they arrived in the tunnel, everyone saw Evan on the ground, crying his eyes out. Josie ran over to him and hugged him, "what happened? Are you okay? Where is Harold?" Josie said, "He's gone Josie…gone…forever…" Evan cried. Josie didn't understand what Evan said, she was in shock and continued to hold Evan tightly. Everyone stood there looking at Evan, anxious to find out what had caused the shockwave and made the creatures disappear.

After a few minutes, Evan stood up and looked at Momma Tree, "I'm so sorry Ms. Tree," he said. Momma Tree looked at him, she knew Harold was going to do something rash when he took the cube and ran into the woods but didn't know what. She walked up to Evan, "It's not your fault, I'm sure you tried to stop him." She said, trying to comfort him. Evan began to cry again, "It all happened…so…fast," he replied. Momma Tree grabbed Evan, hugging him closely. At this moment she had realized that her son was no longer with her and began to cry with Evan.

Everyone else could recognize that something was wrong and that Harold didn't make it. They walked over to Evan and Momma Tree, wrapping their arms around them. Everyone wept, so many things had taken place, so quickly that it almost felt unreal. "Ms. Jackson, Momma Tree, thank you for saving us," Emma said. Momma Tree looked over at Emma and smiled, wiping tears from her eyes. In that moment everyone grasped just how much they all meant to each other.

They all had stopped crying, "well kids, I guess we might as well check on everyone else and go clean up the mess," Momma Tree said, trying to pull herself together. Everyone agreed while they slowly gathered themselves. Josie grabbed Evans' hand and they led everyone back up to the field. Once they reached the field, they saw all of their weapons and picked them back up to bring them home. "Okay kids…I will see you later," Momma tree said abruptly before walking to her home. Everyone felt her pain and couldn't help but watch her walk away.

Josie, Evan and David decided to run back to Josie and David's house to check on their parents. "Ms. Jackson, do you need help cleaning up?" Emma asked, "thank you, but I should be okay, you should get home and check on your parents. Same with you Charleston and Noah," Ms. Jackson replied. The kids all listened to her, running back home waving goodbye. Ms. Jackson wiped her forehead, taking a deep breath before walking back to her home.

David ran through the front door of his house, "mom!" He said, "David! You're safe" she cheered, running at him hugging him and kissing his cheek. Josie and Evan stayed outside, holding each other's hands. "Where did Harold go?" Josie asked hesitantly, "He put the cube back in its place…and…poof he was gone." Evan replied with sadness in his eyes. Josie sighed, "He kept us all safe by doing what he did," Josie said, leaning into comfort Evan. They said their goodbyes and Evan ran back to his home.

Momma Tree arrived at her house and walked in through the back door. She was so proud of Harold for sacrificing himself to save everyone, but she wanted to hug him one last time. She walked in Harold's room and saw the letter he had written on his desk; she picked it up. Every word she read she could hear Harold's voice; she smiled and a tear fell from her left eye. She hugged the letter close to her heart then laid down on Harold's bed and began to fall asleep.

Down the road Ms. Jackson was gathering up the remaining pieces of broken glass on her floor. She was sad but thankful to be home. After the final dustpan was full of glass, she felt ready to make her way to bed. She went to her bedroom and saw snuggles in his favorite sleeping spot. She cuddled up next to him for comfort while nodding off.

The rest of the town had finished cleaning their homes for the night. There wasn't anything left to do but make their way to bed and return to cleaning tomorrow. The kids were finally getting into bed, some of them crying while staying up and others being so tired they fell asleep instantly. In one oppressing night, the town had finally felt normal again.

The next morning everyone got up as soon as the sun rose. Sounds of Blue Jays and Cardinals filled the outside air, restoring life to a dulled town. It was as if the wildlife had been suppressed the entire time leading up to last night.

Momma Tree had woken up with Harold's blanket pulled over her. She put the note back down on his desk and made her way to the kitchen for a cup of coffee. She glanced outside and saw the birds outside and smiled. At this point she accepted what had happened to her son and no longer believed in being sad. After all, what Harold did was valiant and noble.

Momma Tree decided that today would be a good day to gather everyone and have a celebration of life for Harold. She put on a fresh shirt and pants, then put on her slippers with her coffee in hand and started knocking on doors. "Hello Huffington's, I just wanted to let you know, I'm going to be having a celebration of life for Harold in the field at one." She said, "I'm so sorry for your loss miss Tree, we will be there," said Mrs. Huffington. Momma Tree took a swig of her coffee walking away and moving onto the next door.

Josie and Emma were cleaning up remainders of misplaced mulch and garden edging at Josie's house. They had already gotten the news about Harold's celebration of life and were in good spirits. "You and Evan huh?" Emma said while smirking, Josie smiled back, "Yes, he's so dreamy," she replied. "I'm happy for you girl, I'm glad he finally had the guts to tell you," Emma said. Josie had pure joy written all over her face and continued to throw mulch back into the garden.

The time was near twelve thirty and everyone rushed to get ready for Harold's celebration of life. Josie put on her dazzling dress, hoping to impress Evan. Momma tree had set up a table with Harold's guitar and pictures of him. She had rows of chairs that Ms. Jackson had grabbed from the school for her. It was almost one fifteen until everyone had shown up and sat down.

Momma Tree waited for people to get situated before starting her speech. "I would just like to say thank you for coming, I'm sure Harold can feel all the love you all share. What can I say about my boy, he was the most loving person I have ever known. Every day I came home from work, he would let me know how beautiful I am and how much he loved me. He had a way with people that let him get along with just about anyone. He was smart, funny and full of life. I can't believe he saved all of us. He sacrificed his life and I will forever be thankful to him for that." She started to cry and all of Harold's friends joined her at the table.

Emma comforted Momma Tree while she was crying. "I just want to say, my man Harold was the coolest bro I ever had. I will never forget him," Noah said. "We wouldn't be here today if he didn't make the plan to hold the line, he empowered us to keep fighting," Charleston said. Josie made her way to the front, "Harold showed me what a leader should be like. He never looked scared and stood tall no matter what," Josie cried, hugging Momma Tree.

All of the kids began to cry with Momma Tree. They huddled up closely, "We Miss you Harold, we love you," Emma shouted while crying hysterically. Evan wiped his tears and grabbed Harold's guitar off of the table. He snuck back into the middle of the group and stood near Momma Tree. He raised Harold's guitar high to the sky and chanted, "FRIENDS…FOREVER!"

About The Author

DAKOTA SHALINS is the author of Castle of Pine. He grew up in a small town in Maine. He always had a creative side, writing short stories as a child. When he was younger he pursued music, songwriting, producing, and audio engineering. He continues to write fantasy books and will be releasing more soon.